THE PATH TO HER HEART

THE PATH TO HER HEART

LINDA FORD

THORNDIKE
CHIVERS

LIBRARY OF CONGRESS CATALOGING-IN-PUBLICATION DATA

Ford, Linda.
   The path to her heart / by Linda Ford.
     p. cm. — (Thorndike Press large print Christian romance)
   ISBN-13: 978-1-4104-1985-9 (alk. paper)
   ISBN-10: 1-4104-1985-1 (alk. paper)
   1. Depressions—1929—Fiction. 2. Nurses—Fiction. 3.
Man-woman relationships—Fiction. 4. Large type books. I.
Title.
PS3556.O71255P38 2009
813'.54—dc22   2009022173

BRITISH LIBRARY CATALOGUING-IN-PUBLICATION DATA AVAILABLE

Published in 2009 in the U.S. by arrangement with Harlequin Books S.A.
Published in 2010 in the U.K. by arrangement with Harlequin Enterprises II B.V.

U.K. Hardcover: 978 1 408 45724 5 (Chivers Large Print)
U.K. Softcover: 978 1 408 45725 2 (Camden Large Print)

Printed in the United States of America
1 2 3 4 5 6 7 13 12 11 10 09

Jesus Christ the same yesterday, and to day, and for ever.

— *Hebrews* 13:8

To my friend, Alma, who has always
been such a
faithful encourager in my faith walk.

CHAPTER ONE

Favor, South Dakota
1934

They represented all she wanted.

They were everything she could never have.

The pair caught twenty-four-year-old Emma Spencer's attention as she made her way home. The way the tall man bent to the sweet little boy at his side, the tenderness in his gesture as he adjusted the child's hat and straightened his tweed coat brought a sting of unexpected tears to her eyes.

The child said something, and the man squatted to eye level, took the boy's chin between long fingers and smiled as he answered. Even from where she stood, Emma could see strong and assuring depths in his dark eyes. Then he straightened, his expression determined, and stared across the street.

Emma ducked, afraid he'd notice her

interest and think her unduly curious. But she couldn't resist a guarded look at the pair.

The boy took the man's hand. The man picked up a battered suitcase and they continued on.

Emma's throat closed so tightly that she struggled to breathe. An ache as wide as the Dakota prairies sucked at her thoughts. Just a few steps away, across the wind-swept, dusty street, stood the embodiment of all she longed for — a strong, caring man and a dear little child. She mentally shook herself. Although it was not to be, she had no reason to begrudge the fact. She loved being a nurse. She loved helping people. Most of all, she had a responsibility to her parents and brother, struggling to survive the drought and Depression on the farm back home. They depended on the money she sent from her wages each month. She thought of her brother, Sid, and drew in a steadying breath to stop a shiver of guilt. She waited for her lungs to ease and let her usually buried dreams subside into wispy clouds she knew would drift across her thoughts from time to time, like the straw-colored autumn leaves skittering past her feet.

The pair turned in at Ada Adams's boardinghouse and stopped at the front door, side-by-side, tall and straight as two soldiers. She smiled at the way the boy glanced at the man to see if he imitated the stance correctly.

The door opened. Gray-haired Ada reached out and hugged them each in turn, then drew them inside.

Emma gasped and halted her journey toward the boardinghouse. This must be the nephew — a widower — Ada expected. Somehow Emma anticipated an older man with a much older son. Truthfully, Emma had paid little attention when Ada made the announcement of their impending arrival. She'd simply been relieved Ada finally decided to get help running the house. The work was far too much for the older woman, suffering from arthritis. Now Emma wished she'd thought to have asked some questions. How old was the man? How old his son? How long was he staying? What had Ada said happened to his wife? Ada might have answered all her questions but Emma had been dashing out the door and hadn't stopped to listen to the whole story.

Emma hesitated, calming her too eager desire to follow this pair. She glanced at her sturdy white shoes. Her white uniform revealed the evidence of a hard day at the hospital. The weather had been cool when she left before dawn and she'd worn her woolen cape, but now the sun shone warmly and she carried her cape over her arm.

She needed a few minutes to collect her thoughts and seek a solution to this sudden yearning. Rather than cross to the boarding-house, she continued along the sidewalk with no destination in mind, simply the need to think in solitude.

She passed yards enclosed by picket fences. Mr. Blake fussed about his flower beds, preparing them to survive a bitter South Dakota winter. She called a greeting and he waved.

Praying silently, she circled the block. *Lord, God, You know the road before me. You know I don't resent my responsibility. In fact, I am grateful as can be for this job and the chance to help my parents. It's only occasionally I wish for things that might have been. This is one of those times. I thought I had dealt with my disappointment and buried my dreams, but it seems they don't have the decency to stay dead and buried. Yet I will not fret about it. I know You will give me the strength to do what I must. In Thee do I rejoice. Blessed be Your name.*

A smile curved her lips as peace flooded her heart. She knew what she had to do, how she had to face the future, and she would gladly do it.

Her resolve restored, she walked back to the boardinghouse. Only for a second did her feet falter as she remembered Ada's nephew's dark eyes and the way he smiled at his small son. A tiny sound of disgust escaped her lips. She wasn't one to let fanciful notions fill her head. No. She was the kind to do what had to be done. No one and nothing would divert her from her responsibilities. She tipped her thoughts back to her prayer. God would help her. Yet, it might prove prudent to avoid as much contact with the nephew as possible. Certainly they would sit around the same table for meals but apart from that . . .

She suddenly chuckled. The man might be unbearably rude or snobbish, even if in those few moments as he encouraged his son, he'd touched her heart.

Her smile flattened. Rogue or otherwise, she needn't worry. He'd probably not even notice her. She was no china doll. Her eyes should have been blue to go with her blond hair. Instead she had dark brown eyes, equally dark lashes and brows. Too often people gave her a strange look as if startled by the contrast. She'd been told many times it gave her a look of determination — a woman more suited for work than romance. Yet . . .

She pushed away useless dreams, straightened her shoulders and stepped into the warm house.

She thought of slipping up the stairs to change, but she would only be avoiding the inevitable. Sooner or later she'd have to meet the man. Besides, despite the rumpled state of her uniform, wearing it made her feel strong and competent. A glance in the hall mirror, a tuck of some loose strands of hair into her thick bun and she headed into the kitchen.

He stood with his back to her. He'd shed his coat. He was thin as were many people after years of drought and Depression prices. His shoulders were wide and square, and he was even taller than she'd thought — six foot or better, if she didn't miss her guess. His hair was brown as a warm mink coat.

She blamed the hot cookstove for the way her cheeks stung with heat.

Ada leaned to the right so she could see past her nephew. "Emma, I told you my nephew, Boothe, was coming."

The man faced her. His eyes weren't dark as she first thought; they only appeared so because they were deep-set and gray as a winter sky, filling her heart with a raging storm to rival any blizzard she'd ever experienced.

"Boothe Wallace." Ada's voice came like a faint call on a breeze as Emma's emotions ran the gamut of longing, loneliness and finally into self-disgust that she couldn't better control her thoughts.

"Boothe, this is one of my guests, Emma Spencer."

Emma, her feelings firmly under control, stepped forward but halted as his expression grew forbidding.

His gaze raced over her uniform, pausing at the blotch where she'd tried to erase evidence of a young patient's vomit.

She wished she'd taken the time to change. "I'm sorry," she murmured, forcing the words past the blockage in her throat. "I just got off work."

"A nurse." Boothe's words carried a condemning tone, though Emma could think of no reason for it. She'd given him no cause to object to anything she'd done or not done.

"She works at the hospital," Ada explained. "And this little fellow is Boothe's son, Jessie."

Boothe showed no sign of moving over to allow Emma to meet the boy, so she stepped sideways. Jessie perched on the table. He gave her a shy, glancing smile, allowing her a glimpse of startlingly blue eyes. She wanted to sweep the adorable child into her arms. She wisely restrained herself. She loved working with children best. Her superiors praised her rapport with them.

The boy wore an almost new shirt of fine cotton and knickers of good quality wool. Compared to his father's well-worn clothes, Jessie was dressed like a prince.

"I'm happy to meet you, Jessie," she said in the soft tone she reserved for children and frightened patients. "How old are you?"

He darted another glance at her and smiled so wide she ached to ruffle his sandy-colored hair. "Six." His voice had a gritty sound as if he wanted everyone to forget he was a little boy and think he was a man.

That's when she saw the deep slash on his arm and the blood-soaked rag that had recently been removed. "You've been hurt. What happened?" Instinctively, she stepped forward, intent on examining the wound.

"Ran into a sticking out nail. Daddy got really mad at the man pushing the cart." He gave the cut a look, shuddered and turned away, but not before she got a glimpse of his tears. The wound had to hurt like fury. It was deep and gaping, but a few stitches

16

would fix it up and he'd heal neatly as long as he didn't get an infection — and unless it was properly cleaned, he stood a good chance of just that. Dirt blackened the edges of the cut. "I'll clean it for you, and then your father can take you to the doctor."

But before she reached Jessie's side, Boothe stepped in front of her.

"No doctor. No nurse." His harsh tone sent a shudder along Emma's spine. "I'll take care of him myself." His stubborn stance was a marked contrast to the tenderness he'd exhibited a short time ago on the street.

She thought she must have misunderstood him. "It needs cleaning and stitching. I can do the former but a good doctor should do the latter." Again she moved to take over the chore.

Again he blocked her. "I'll be the one taking care of my son."

The challenge in his eyes felt like a spear to her heart, but she wouldn't let it deter her. "Your son needs medical attention."

"I don't need the bungling interference of either a doctor or a nurse." He'd lowered his voice so only Emma heard him.

She recoiled from the venomous accusation. "I do *not* bungle."

He held his hand toward her, palm forward, effectively forbidding her to go any farther.

She clasped her hands at her waist, squeezed her fingers hard enough to hurt and clamped her mouth shut to stop the angry protest. How dare this man judge her incompetent! But even more, how could he ignorantly, stubbornly, put his son at risk? Too many times she'd seen the sorry result of home remedies. She'd seen children suffer needlessly because their parents refused to take them to the doctor until their injuries or illnesses pushed them to the verge of death. She shuddered, recalling some who came too late.

He turned back to his aunt. "Would you have a basin?"

Ada's eyes were wary as if wondering if she should intervene then she gave a barely perceptible shrug, pulled one from the cupboard and handed it to him.

Boothe's demanding gaze forbade Emma to interfere. When he seemed confident she'd stand back, he turned to his son. "Jessie, I'm going to clean this and then I'll bandage it."

Boothe filled a basin as Emma helplessly looked on. It took a great deal of self-discipline to stand by when little Jessie sent her a frightened look as if begging her to

18

promise everything would be okay. Unfortunately, she couldn't give such assurance. The wound continued to bleed. One good thing about the flow of blood — it served to cleanse the deeper tissues.

Boothe dipped a clean cloth in the water. Jessie whimpered. "Now, son. I won't hurt you any more than I need to. You know that?"

Jessie nodded and blinked back tears.

"You be a brave man and this will be done sooner than you know."

Jessie pressed his lips together and nodded again.

Emma admired the little boy's bravery. She watched with hawk-like concentration as Boothe cleaned the edges of the wound. He did a reasonably good job but it didn't satisfy Emma. She itched to pour on a good dose of disinfectant. Iodine was her first choice. She'd never seen a wound infect if it'd been properly doused with the potent stuff. She opened her mouth to make a suggestion but Boothe's warning glance made her swallow back the words. The boy would have a terrible scar without stitches, and the wound would keep bleeding for an unnecessarily long time.

"Aunt Ada, do you have a clean rag?" Boothe asked. Ada handed him an old sheet.

No, Emma mentally screamed. *At least use something sterile.* "I could get dressings from the hospital," she offered, ignoring his frown.

"This will do just fine." He tore the fabric into strips.

Anger, like hot coals to her heart, surged through her. How could this man be so stubborn? Why did he resist medical help with such blindness?

Ignoring her, though he couldn't help but be aware of her scowling concern, he pressed the edges of the wound together and wrapped it securely with the cloth, fixing the end in place with the pin Ada handed him then stepped back, pleased with his work.

Emma watched the bandage, knowing it would soon pinken with blood. By the time Boothe had washed and cleaned up, the telltale pink was the size of a quarter. She could be silent no longer. "Without stitches it will continue to bleed. You need to take him to the doctor."

Boothe, drying his hands on a kitchen towel, shot her a look fit to sear her skin. "We do not need or want to see a doctor. They do more harm than good."

Emma shifted her gaze to Jessie, saw his eyes wide with what she could only assume was fear. Her insides settled into hardness. "May I speak with you privately?" She addressed Boothe, well aware of Ada's tight smile and Jessie's stark stare.

"I don't think that's necessary."

"I do." She moved to the doorway and waited for him to join her in the hall. She wondered if he would simply ignore her, but with a resigned sigh, he strode across the room, his movements and expression saying he hoped it wouldn't take long, because he was only doing his best to avoid a scene.

She went to the front door so their conversation wouldn't be overheard in the kitchen. "I am deeply concerned about your attitude toward the medical profession. Not only does it prevent you from taking your son to the doctor for needed care but it is instilling in him an unnecessary and potentially dangerous fear of doctors. There could come a time when it is a matter of life or death that he seek medical attention." She couldn't shake her initial response to the man, couldn't stop herself from being attracted to his looks, his demeanor and his gentleness toward his son. Yet he was ignorant and stubborn about medical things — the sort of man who normally filled her with undiluted anger.

"Do you realize this is none of your business?"

She didn't answer. A person didn't interfere with how a man raised his children — one of the unwritten laws of their society. But she could not, *would* not, stand by silently while someone was needlessly put at risk. *Never again.*

He suddenly leaned closer, his gray eyes as cold as a prairie winter storm. "I've seen firsthand the damage medical people inflict. I will not subject my son to that."

She drew back, startled by his vehemence. "Our goal is to help and heal, not damage."

His nostrils flared, his eyes narrowed. He sucked in air like someone punched him. "My wife is dead because of medical 'help.' "

His words filtered through her senses as shock, surprise, sympathy and sorrow mixed together. "I'm —"

"Don't bother trying to defend them."

She had been about to express her sympathy not defend a situation she knew nothing about, but he didn't seem to care to hear anything from her and rushed on.

"They poisoned her. Pure and simple. Overdosed her with quinine. The judge ruled it accidental. He reprimanded them for carelessness, but they got away with murder. So you see —" he took a deep breath and settled back on his heels "— I have good reason to avoid the medical profession and good reason to teach my son to do so as well."

Emma wondered why quinine had been prescribed. It was often used to treat fevers or irregular heartbeats. Adverse reactions were common but reversible. Although she'd never seen toxicity, she knew it involved heart problems as well as seizures and coma. How dreadful to see it happen to a loved one. And so needless. An attentive nurse should have picked up the symptoms immediately.

Determined not to let her tears surface, Emma widened her eyes. "I'm sorry. It should have never happened. But it's not fair to think all of us are careless."

"Do you think I'm going to take a chance?"

They faced each other. His eyes looked as brittle as hers felt. He was wrong in thinking he couldn't trust another doctor or nurse. It put both himself and Jessie at risk. But she didn't have to read minds to know he wasn't about to be convinced otherwise. Her shoulders sagged as she gave up the idea of trying. "I'm sorry about your loss, but aren't you spreading blame a little too thick and wide? Allowing it to cloud your judgment?"

He snorted. "I realize we are destined to live in the same house and I intend to be civil. But I warn you not to interfere with how I raise my son."

Emma scooped her cape off the banister and headed up the stairs, her emotions fluctuating between anger and pity. But she had to say something. Her conscience would not allow her to ignore the situation. She turned. "Sometimes, Mr. Wallace, a person has to learn to trust or he puts himself and others at risk."

Boothe made an explosive sound. His expression grew thunderous.

Emma met his look without flinching. There was no reason she should want to reach out and smooth away the harsh lines in his face. Except, she reluctantly admitted, her silly reaction to a little scene on the sidewalk.

"Trust." He snorted. "From here on out, I trust no one." He pursed his lips. "No one."

He'd been badly hurt. But he verged on becoming bitter. Silently, she prayed for wisdom to say the right thing. "Not even God?" She spoke softly.

He stood rigid as a fence post for a moment then his shoulders sank. "I'm trying to trust Him." His head down, he headed back to the kitchen.

"I will pray for you, Boothe Wallace."

CHAPTER TWO

Boothe stayed out of sight of the kitchen door to compose himself. Jessie had enough fears to deal with without seeing his father upset. He hoped seeing Emma in her nurse's uniform wouldn't remind Jessie of that awful time two years ago when Alyse had been murdered by a negligent doctor. Aided and abetted by a belligerent nurse. The doctor said it would stop her fluttering heartbeat that left her weak. Instead, it had succeeded in stopping her heart completely. The judge might have ruled the incident accidental, but Boothe considered it murder. There was no other word for giving a killing dose of medicine. Alyse hadn't stood a chance. He shuddered back the memory of her violent seizures.

And for Emma to suggest he should trust! She didn't know the half of it. He'd trusted too easily. It cost him his wife. No. He would not trust again. Ever.

Not even God? Her words rang through his head. Even trusting God had grown difficult. One thing forced him to make the choice to do so — Jessie. He feared for his son's safety if God didn't protect him. Hopefully, his trust would not be misplaced. *Trust in the Lord with all thine heart; and lean not unto thine own understanding. In all thy ways acknowledge Him, and He shall direct thy paths.* He knew the words well. However, reciting verses was far easier than having the assurance the words promised.

He drew in a deep breath. Why hadn't Aunt Ada warned him one of her guests was a nurse? But then what difference would it have made? Leaving Lincoln, Nebraska, and moving to South Dakota had been the only way to escape the threat he faced back in the city of losing Jessie. Besides, there was no work back there and he'd been evicted from his shabby apartment. Here Jessie was safe with him. He could put up with an interfering nurse for Jessie's sake. He would forget about Emma and the way her brown eyes melted with gentleness one moment and burned with fury the next. He smiled knowing he'd annoyed her as much as she annoyed him. Why that should amuse him, he couldn't say. But it did.

He paused outside the kitchen.

"Where did my daddy go?" His son's voice had a brittle edge signaling his distress. Poor Jessie had dealt with far too much in the past two years, but these past two weeks had been especially upsetting with losing their home and then being snatched away from his Aunt Vera and Uncle Luke. Jessie did not understand the reasons behind this sudden move. But it had been unavoidable. Trusting his sister-in-law had almost proven a disaster. Boothe only hoped Favor would be far enough from Lincoln.

Aunt Ada, bless her heart, answered Jessie soothingly. "He's just in the other room. He'll be back shortly."

"Is my daddy mad?"

Aunt Ada chuckled. "I can't say for sure, but I don't think it's anything we need to worry about."

"Is my arm going to fall off?"

Boothe stepped into the room intent on reassuring his son. The bandage already needed changing. "Your arm is going to be all right." He kept all traces of anger from his voice even though he silently blamed Emma for frightening Jessie.

"But that lady —"

"Emma?" Aunt Ada prompted.

"Yes, Emma —"

"*Miss* Emma to you," Boothe said.

"Miss Emma. She's a nurse. She said —"

"I'll wrap your arm better. It will be just fine." *Thank you, Miss Emma, for alarming an innocent child.* He gently took off the soiled dressing, tore up more strips and created a pad. "Aunt Ada, do you have adhesive tape?"

"In the left-hand drawer." She pointed toward the cupboard. He found the tape and cut several pieces, using them to close the edges of the cut before he applied the pad. He wrapped it with fresh lengths of the old sheet and pinned the end. "There. You'll soon be good as new."

Jessie nodded, his blue gaze bright. "I don't need a doctor, do I?"

Boothe kept his voice steady despite the anger twitching at his insides. "Jessie, my boy, a man does not run to the doctor every time he gets a cut. Okay?"

"Okay." He slid his gaze to Aunt Ada. "Miss Emma lives here?"

"Yes. Did you like her?"

"She has a nice smile."

Boothe shot Aunt Ada a warning glance. "Where do you want us to put our stuff?"

Aunt Ada winked at Boothe. "She's a nice woman. Knows her own mind. I admire that in a person."

Jessie nodded vigorously. "Me, too."

Boothe grabbed the suitcase, wanting nothing more than to end this conversation. He did not want Jessie getting interested in Emma.

"I've made space for you in the back of the storeroom. Sorry I can't offer you a bedroom but the upstairs ones are all rented, for which I thank God. And I don't intend to give up mine."

"I'm sure we'll be more than comfortable." Boothe fell in beside Aunt Ada as she limped toward the back of the kitchen. Jessie followed on his heels.

The room was large, full of cupboards stacked with canned goods, bottles of home preserves, tins and sacks of everything from oats to bay leaves. Spicy, homey smells filled the air. He tightened his jaw, remembering when such aromas, such sights, meant home. With forced determination he finished his visual inspection of the room. Two narrow side-by-side cots and a tall dresser fit neatly along the far wall. A window with a green shade rolled almost to the top gave natural light. "This is more than adequate. Thank you."

"Is this our place?" Jessie asked.

"For as long as you want," Aunt Ada said.

A load of weight slid from Boothe's shoulders. They would be safe here. And maybe one day in the unforeseeable future, they might even be happy again. "I can't thank you enough."

Jessie kicked off his boots, plopped down on one bed, his bony knees crooked toward the ceiling. "I had a room of my own at Auntie Vera's."

Boothe had been forced to leave Jessie with Vera on school days and often on weekends as he tried to find enough work to make ends meet. He hadn't liked it, though he appreciated that Jessie had a safe place to stay.

He hadn't expected it to be a complete mistake.

"No thanks needed." Ada grinned at him. "You'll be earning your keep sure enough. Things have been neglected of late. I can't get around like I used to."

"I'm here to help. Tell me what you need done."

"I'd appreciate if you look after the furnace first. Emma's been kind enough to do it but she's a paying guest."

"I'll tend to it. Jessie, your books and toys are in the suitcase. I'll be back in a few minutes."

Jessie bolted to his feet and scrambled into his boots, ignoring the dragging laces as he scurried after Boothe.

Boothe should have known the boy wouldn't let him out of his sight. He squatted down to face Jessie. "I don't want you to come downstairs with me." He had no idea what condition the cellar was in. It might not be safe for a six-year-old. "You go with Aunt Ada and wait for me. I'll be back as soon as I can."

Jessie's eyes flooded with fear.

Boothe squeezed his son's shoulder. He hated leaving him but Jessie was safe. Sooner or later he'd have to get used to the fact his father had to leave him at times. But he'd learn that Boothe would always return.

Aunt Ada took Jessie's hand. "I have a picture book you might like to see."

Boothe nodded his thanks as his aunt led Jessie back to the kitchen table. Only then did he venture down the worn wooden steps. He found the furnace and fed it, dragged the ashes into the ash pail then looked around the cavernous cellar. Bins built along one side contained potatoes and a variety of root vegetables. He hadn't been to Aunt Ada's in years but as a kid had spent several summers visiting her. He remembered her huge garden in the adjoining lot. But she had been quick and light on her feet back then. Now she moved as if every joint hurt. Did she still grow everything the household consumed?

Boxes were stacked on wide shelves. He opened one and saw a collection of magazines. The next held rags. Another seemed to be full of men's clothes. He couldn't imagine whose they were, seeing as Aunt Ada had never married. Perhaps a guest had left them behind. He pulled out a pair of trousers and held them to his waist. He found a heavy coat, a pair of sagging boots and a variety of shirts. He'd ask Aunt Ada about the things. They were better than anything he owned. Despite his disappointment at Vera's treachery, he allowed himself a moment of gratitude for the fine clothes she bought Jesse.

He carried the pail of ashes upstairs and paused, breathing in the aroma of pork roast and applesauce. The furnace hummed and the warmth of coal heat spread about him. This was a good place to be. Safe and solid. He tilted his head toward the kitchen as he heard Jessie.

"When will my daddy come back?" His voice crackled with tension.

Boothe hurried to the back door to get rid of the ash bucket.

Emma's gentle voice answered Jessie. "Your daddy is taking care of the furnace so

33

you'll stay warm. What did he say when he went to the cellar?"

"He said he'd be back as soon as he could."

"There you go. Even when you can't see him, you can remember what he said."

Boothe stood stock-still as Emma reassured Jessie. A blizzard of emotions raced through him — gratitude that she dealt with Jessie so calmly, soothingly. Anger and frustration that Jessie had to confront the fear of loss. Children his age should be secure in the love of a mother and father. Most of all, emptiness sucked at his gut making him feel as naked, exposed and helpless as a tree torn from the ground by a tornado, roots and all. The future stretched out as barren as the drought-stricken prairies. This was not how he'd envisioned his life. Nope, in his not-so-long-ago plans there'd been a woman who shared his home and made it a welcoming place.

He clenched his jaw so hard his teeth ached. He'd come here to find peace and safety. In the space of half an hour, Emma had robbed him of that, not once, but twice. Thankfully he wouldn't have to see her more than a few minutes each day — only long enough to share a meal with all the boarders.

He deposited the bucket on the flagstone sidewalk where it would be unable to start a fire. The wind made the ashes glow red. Dust sifted across the backyard. Late October often meant snow, which would settle the dust. But this year the snow had not come. Only the endless wind. He lifted his face to the sky. *God, when will this end?* He couldn't say exactly what he meant. The drought? The nationwide Depression? His loneliness? Jessie's fears? He supposed he meant all of them.

Not that he expected divine intervention. Seems a man just did what he could and hoped for the best. He hadn't received what he considered best, or even good, in a long time. He tried to find anything good in his life. Right now, about all he could give that label to was Jessie. He paused . . . and this house. He headed to the kitchen.

Jessie sat at the table, a coloring book and crayons before him, but he paid more attention to Emma than his coloring. Emma stood at the stove stirring something while Aunt Ada carved the pork roast. Emma had changed into a black skirt and pale blue sweater. She glanced up as he stepped into the room and her gaze collided with his. Her dark eyes were a surprising contrast to her golden hair. If he didn't know she was a nurse, he might think her an attractive woman.

He hurried to her side and reached for the spoon. "I've come to help Aunt Ada. Now that I'm here, there's no reason for one of the boarders to work." His voice was harsher than he intended and caused the two women to stare at him.

Jessie stiffened. His eyes grew wide and wary.

"What I meant is you're a paying guest. You shouldn't have to help." He forced a smile to his lips and tried to put a smile in his voice. He knew he failed miserably.

He felt Emma, inches away at his elbow, studying him, but refused to meet her gaze until she laughed and he jerked around in surprise. Her eyes glistened with amusement, and her smile seemed to go on forever. He couldn't breathe as it brushed his heart. He shook his head, angry at himself and his silly imaginations.

"Here you go." She handed him the spoon and a jar full of white liquid. "You do know how to make gravy?" Her words were round with barely restrained laughter.

He looked at the pot of bubbling liquid on the stove and the jar. He had no idea what he was expected to do.

Emma laughed low and sweet, tickling his

insides. He fought his reaction. He could not allow a feeling at such odds with how he felt when he saw her in a nurse's uniform.

She laughed again. "A simple yes or no would suffice."

Behind him Aunt Ada chuckled.

"Daddy, you can make gravy?" Jessie's surprised awe brought more low laughter from Emma.

"I'm sure I could if someone would tell me how."

"Very well," Emma said. "Stir the juice and slowly pour the flour and water mixture in. The trick is to keep it from going lumpy."

Boothe followed the instructions as Emma hovered at his elbow watching him like a hungry eagle waiting for some helpless prey. A reluctant grin tugged at the corners of his mouth. His experience taught him nurses didn't care for anyone showing they might know a thing or two. He'd do this right if only to prove he was as capable as she.

The gravy thickened. "Smells good. How am I doing?"

She stepped back and considered him. "Are you sure you haven't done this before?"

He grinned, glad to have succeeded in the face of her doubt. "Cross my heart."

Aunt Ada laughed. "Maybe you could teach him to mash potatoes, too."

Emma didn't seem the least bit annoyed at his success. In fact, if her flashing smile meant anything, she seemed rather pleased about it.

He couldn't tear his gaze away from hers as something inside him, both exciting and alarming, demanded consideration. His stomach growled and he freed himself from her dark eyes. He was only hungry. Nothing more. "I'm sure I can learn to mash potatoes with the best of them."

Emma handed him a masher and pointed him toward the big pot. Not only was there pork roast, gravy and potatoes but there was a pot of turnips and a bowl of canned tomatoes. His mouth watered at the prospect of so much to eat. For months he'd been forced to ration every scrap of food he scrounged, glad Jessie was being well fed with Vera and Luke. All this abundance was unbelievable. God's blessing? A flash of hope and belief crossed his mind before he focused his attention on Emma's instructions.

"I think everything is ready," Aunt Ada said a few minutes later. "Jessie, do you want to help me ring the bell for supper?"

Jessie bounced off his chair and followed

Ada into the hall. At the bottom of the stairs, she handed him a little brass bell and instructed him to shake it. He laughed at the racket it made. From upstairs came the sound of doors opening.

Emma scooped the potatoes into a bowl and poured the gravy into a large pitcher. "Help me carry in the food." She nodded toward Boothe.

He grabbed the platter of meat in one hand and the gravy jug in the other and followed her into the dining room where the table was already set. He counted nine chairs. That made six paying guests. Quite a load for Aunt Ada. He intended to ease her load and find a job as well. He'd heard there was always work in the town of Favor, on the edge of the irrigation area.

Aunt Ada took her place at one end of the table and indicated Boothe should sit at the other end, Jessie at his right. "As soon as we're all here, I'll make the introductions."

People filed in, taking what seemed to be appointed places. As soon as each chair had a body behind it, Aunt Ada spoke. "I told you all that my nephew, Boothe, agreed to come and help me run the boardinghouse. The young man beside him is his son, Jessie."

Jessie pulled himself to rigid attention at

being called a man.

Boothe grinned. His heart filled with pride.

One by one, Aunt Ada introduced the others starting on her right. "Loretta, one of my oldest and dearest friends."

The older, thin woman smiled at Aunt Ada before she turned to Boothe. "I'm glad you've come."

Beside her stood a woman, probably in her forties, Sarah, who had a dress shop downtown. Next, Betty, a chambermaid at the new hotel, a girl fresh off the farm if Boothe didn't miss his guess. He turned to those on the other side of the table. Beside Jessie stood Don, a man in his late twenties or early thirties, and next to him, Ed, an eager-faced young man who could barely tear his gaze away from Betty long enough to greet Boothe. Both men worked at the brick factory.

And then Emma. She grinned at him. "Boothe made the gravy, so if you have any complaints, direct them to him, not me."

Don chuckled. "Emma's teasing you already. Best be careful. She can have you running in circles."

Boothe kept his expression bland. "I don't run in circles." Maybe not literally but she'd already proved her ability to send his thoughts down useless rabbit trails.

Aunt Ada cleared her throat. "Shall we pray?"

They all bowed as she offered up thanks for the food and for Boothe and Jessie's arrival. Her gratitude soothed away Boothe's tension.

Only then did they sit down.

The meal proved excellent, the conversation interesting. Ed and Don told him of the work in the factory.

"You could probably get a job there," Don said.

"I'll look into it." Boothe planned to check out a few other prospects first.

He expected the boarders would disperse as soon as they finished. Instead, everyone grabbed a handful of things and headed for the kitchen. The women began to wash and dry dishes while Ed and Don shook the tablecloth and arranged the chairs. Boothe tried to keep up but it seemed each knew what he or she was expected to do.

"Aunt Ada certainly has you organized."

"Not Ada," Don said. "She was reluctant to accept help. But when Emma saw how much pain she had, she got us all doing our share."

Emma. Boothe tried to think if it surprised him. She seemed the sort who liked to

41

organize things. Or — his jaw tightened — did she like to be in control? Was it an innate part of being a nurse? Always in control. Always right.

As soon as the dishes were done, the guests moved into the front room. Emma carried in a large tray with a teapot under a knit cozy and cups for everyone. Aunt Ada brought in a plate of cookies. Again, everyone seemed to know what to do. They prepared tea to their liking, served themselves cookies and settled into one of the many chairs. Aunt Ada and Loretta sank into the burgundy couch.

"Do you mind if I give Jessie tea?" Emma asked. She held a cup almost full of milk.

"Can I, Daddy? Please."

Boothe nodded. He sat on one of the upright wooden chairs and edged another close for Jessie.

Emma sat beside the table and pulled a book to her lap. "We've been reading the biography of a missionary to China. You're welcome to join us."

"It will soon be Jessie's bedtime."

"We'll stop when it's time for him to get ready for bed."

Boothe didn't know if he liked the gentle way Emma smiled at his son. He wasn't about to trust another woman getting close to Jessie. He'd learned his lesson, but Jessie's eager expression convinced Boothe to agree to let him stay for the reading.

Loretta and Aunt Ada knitted as Emma read. Sarah sewed lace to a dress. Betty sat, her reddened hands idle, her expression rapt as she followed each word. Both Ed and Don leaned back, simply glad to relax. Emma read well, giving the story lots of drama, and Boothe was drawn into the tale.

Soon Emma closed the book. "End of chapter. I'm going to stop there so Jessie can go to bed."

Boothe jumped up, guilt flooding his thoughts. What kind of father was he to forget his son's bedtime? "Come along, Jessie."

Jessie took his hand but stopped before Emma. "Thank you, Miss Emma. It's a good story. Is it really true?"

"It is. It's exciting to see how God did such wonderful things for them. Doesn't it make you feel safe and loved to know God does the same kinds of things for us?"

Jessie nodded vigorously.

A few minutes later, Boothe tucked him into bed.

"How long do we have to stay here?"

Boothe smoothed the covers over the small body. "I already told you. We're going to live here."

Jessie's eyes were dull with sleep yet he had enough energy to flash his angry displeasure. "Auntie Vera said we could live with her." His words quivered. "I want to live with her and Uncle Luke. I want to go home."

"This is home now. Besides, if we leave, you won't be able to hear the rest of Miss Emma's story." Boothe couldn't believe he'd used Emma as a reason to stay. *Only for Jessie's sake.*

Jessie rubbed his arm and gave Boothe a watery, defiant look. "My arm hurts. I want Auntie Vera."

Alarm snaked up Boothe's spine. Were Jessie's cheeks flushed? Was he fevered? He pressed his palm to his son's forehead. Did he seem warm? Boothe didn't know.

He pulled the covers down and looked at the dressing. A spot of pink stained it. He touched the skin on either side of the white cloth. Did it seem hot? Or was it simply warm from Jessie having his arm under the covers?

Boothe eased the blanket back to Jessie's chin. He had Emma to thank for stirring up unnecessary fears. The wound would heal just fine. Jessie was safer without the interference of any nurse or doctor.

He'd seen Emma eye Jessie's arm several times throughout the meal and afterward. She would do well to respect his wishes for his son. He would not allow an interfering woman — no matter how kind she seemed — to put his child at risk. Nor let his heart wish things could be different.

CHAPTER THREE

Her bedroom lay in late fall darkness. Emma rolled over, turned on her bedside lamp, pulled her Bible to her chest and read a few verses. She prayed for her parents and her brother. *Lord, make sure they're warm and have enough to eat.* Last winter they'd run low on coal and used it so sparingly that the house was always cold. While she was grateful for a warm, safe place to live, she felt guilty knowing Sid and her parents did not enjoy the same luxuries.

As soon as she finished her prayers, she'd run down to the basement and stir up the furnace. She paused. Was the house already warm? Had Boothe already stoked up the fire? How pleasant to waken to a warm room. She returned to her prayers, bringing her patients before God. A couple had been in the hospital for several weeks, fighting dust pneumonia. *Lord, a good snowfall would put an end to the dust. But You know that.*

Just as You know everything we need. She prayed for friends and neighbors. Finally, when she couldn't put it off any longer, she prayed for Boothe. There was something about him that upset her equilibrium. She didn't like it. *Lord, help him learn to trust again. And heal Jessie's wound.* She'd heard Jessie crying in the night. It was all she could do not to run down and check on him. That wound was nasty and no doubt painful. But Boothe had forbidden her to do anything for his son.

She took time to thank God for all the good things in her life. Unable to avoid the truth, she thanked her Lord for Boothe. *He's an answer to prayer for Ada, even though he is certainly not the man I would have sent to help. But again, You know best. Perhaps he needs something he will find here.*

She jumped from bed, dashed across the hall to the washroom and splashed water over her face. Back in her room she pulled on white stockings, slipped into her uniform and pinned a clean apron on top. She toed into her white shoes, tied them neatly then headed downstairs to help Ada with breakfast.

At the kitchen door, she halted.

Boothe presided over the stove, frying bacon. Ada tended to the toast. A pot of coffee bubbled. Emma turned to the dining room, intent on setting the table. She stopped at the doorway. "The table's set."

"Boothe did it," Ada said. "He's catching on quickly."

"I noticed the house is already warm. That's nice." Emma glanced at Boothe. He looked smug as if expecting he'd surprised her.

She shifted her gaze away. She wasn't sure what to do with herself nor where to look, and headed for the window. The square of light revealed the yellowed grass scattered with dried leaves. Emma shivered then turned to catch Boothe watching her.

"It's going to be cold today." He offered her a cup of coffee.

She took it and cradled her hands around its warmth. "I heard Jessie in the night. Is he okay?"

"He's sleeping. I'll leave him until he needs to get ready for school."

"Was his cut hurting him?"

Boothe glowered at her. "He had a nightmare. It will take him a few days to feel secure here."

"It's got to be hard for him." Losing his mother and moving to a strange place. "But please keep an eye on that wound. Infection can be deadly."

"I know enough to take care of my son without your help, if you don't mind." His expression grew darker but she refused to be intimidated. As a nurse, she faced disagreeable patients and families and dealt with them kindly, realizing their anger wasn't directed at her personally. Only with Boothe, it felt personal. She smiled as much to calm herself as to convey kindness to Boothe. She would act professionally even with a man who despised her profession.

The boarders trickled in for breakfast. Loretta never joined them. She had no reason to be up so early. The others gathered round the table, for the most part eating without speaking.

"No snow. That's good," Betty said. "Do you know how much mess snow makes on the floors?" She seemed to be the only one who woke up bright and cheerful.

"Snow would settle the dust and perhaps end the drought."

Emma jerked her head up at Boothe's soft voice, surprised by the emotion hidden in his words. His eyes darkened as he looked deep into her soul. She felt a connection, a shared sorrow at the sad state of the economy, an acknowledgment that life was difficult. Then he shuttered his feelings and his brow furrowed as if she'd overstepped some boundary.

She turned back to her breakfast. He didn't need to fear she'd be intruding into his life. She had more important things to attend to. Besides, she did not want to feel a connection to this man. He was dismissive almost to the point of rudeness and refused medical attention for his son. He'd branded her and the whole medical society because of a terrible accident. Tears stung her eyes at the stupidity that caused the death of his wife. She blinked them away and forced her thoughts to other things — like her responsibilities. She would do all she could to make life more tolerable for Sid and their parents.

Don spoke, thankfully pulling her from her troubled thoughts. "Boothe, did you want me to ask about a job at the factory?"

"Not yet but thanks for offering. I'm hoping to find a job that allows me to be home until Jessie leaves for school. I don't expect I'll be able to be home right after, but I'm grateful Aunt Ada will be here."

The smile he sent his aunt filled Emma with alarming confusion. A man of such contrasts, full of tenderness to his son, warmth to his aunt, cold disapproval to Emma.

Betty jumped up and gathered her dishes.

"Gotta run."

Ed followed hard on her heels. Emma grinned after the pair. Ed moved in a couple months ago, fresh off a dried out farm, and had fallen instantly in love with Betty. Betty, although kind to the boy, did not encourage him. She vowed she'd spent enough years on a farm and stuck in a small town. As soon as she saved enough money, she was off to the city.

Boothe asked Don about other job possibilities. He spoke in an easy, relaxed manner, his tone warm, his expression interested.

Emma's errant thoughts repeated her initial reaction at her first glimpse of him approaching the boardinghouse. *A strong, caring man.* She slammed a mental door. She had her duties. They excluded useless dreams, especially ones that included a man. Emma sobered. She would not let herself be another Ed, longing for something that was impossible.

"Don't worry about the dishes," Ada said as Emma hesitated at the sink. "Boothe will help me."

"Do you want me to bring up a basin of potatoes?" She normally brought whatever vegetables Ada needed to prepare during the day.

"Boothe will do it. I expect to make him work for his keep." Ada's voice held a teasing note.

Emma realized how good this arrangement would be for Ada.

"I'll see you later, then." She wrapped her cape about her and headed out into the cold darkness. The sun breathed pink air over the horizon as she entered the hospital.

At the end of her shift, Emma hurried back to the boardinghouse, shivering in the cold wind and coughing in protest of the dust particles in the air. The endless dust grew tiresome. It would be worse for Mom and Dad and Sid on the farm. Relentless. *God, please send snow. Please end the drought.*

She was getting home later than she should have been thanks to the demands of her job. And she was exhausted — more so in mind than body. It had been one of those days that made her wish she could change people's thoughts.

Two elderly patients died — their deaths not entirely unexpected, but the woman might have survived if she hadn't refused to see a doctor until she was too weak to protest when her daughter insisted she must.

And then a woman came in to have her

baby. She'd been in labor seventy-two hours before she finally decided she needed medical intervention. The baby had been delivered and both were alive, but Emma wondered about the long-term effects on the baby. The infant girl had been slow to start breathing and seemed sluggish in her responses.

Emma wished she could erase the mental images of the worst scene of all — a young man who had been ill for some time but only when he could no longer respond did his parents decide to seek help. By then the skin on the young man hung like a sheet draped over a wooden rack. His eyes were sunken. She couldn't help thinking of Sid, remembering how vigorous he'd been at that age. She smiled past tears. Sid had been so eager for life and adventure — with an attitude that led him to take reckless chances just for a thrill. She stilled a shudder. The consequences of taking such risks had gone beyond harmless adventure.

She'd worked feverishly over the young man in her care, determined she would not let his life slip away. He showed little improvement, even with all her efforts.

Later, in private, Dr. Phelps shook his head. "He's so dehydrated I wonder if his kidneys are even functional."

"I don't understand why people wait so long to get help." Emma's voice was sharp with frustration. "So much of this suffering is unnecessary."

Dr. Phelps sighed. "The greatest disease of all is ignorance."

The young man had still been alive, struggling for each breath, when she'd finally left the hospital, chased away by the matron who insisted Emma was of no value to them if she wore herself out.

Emma paused before the front door of the boardinghouse. She would not drag her frustration and sorrow into the house. *Lord, take my concerns and replace them with Your peace.* She waited until she had a sense of God's comforting arms about her then stepped inside.

From the kitchen came the sound of Jessie's crackling voice, high with some protest and Boothe's lower, calmer response.

As Emma headed for the stairs, she could hear the conversation more clearly.

"Daddy, I want to go home." The irritable note in Jessie's voice alerted Emma's instincts.

"This is home now." Boothe explained in gentle tones with just an edge of impatience.

Emma smiled, guessing this conversation

had gone on for some time and Boothe had about reached the end of his rope.

"I don't like it here." No mistaking Jessie's stubbornness. "I don't like the school. I don't like anything." She heard a small thump, as if Jessie kicked something.

Emma hesitated part way up the stairs, curious to know how Boothe would handle this.

"You'll learn to like it. You'll learn to be happy."

"No. I won't."

Emma tilted her head toward the kitchen. Obviously, Jessie was finding the transition difficult, but it sounded like more than that. He sounded like a child who wasn't feeling well.

She wanted to check on him, but Boothe had made it doubly clear he would tolerate no interference with his son, yet she could simply not ignore the needs of a sick child. Remembering the young man at the hospital, remembering an earlier time when she'd failed to intervene, she spared a moment to pray for wisdom then headed back down the stairs and into the kitchen, not giving herself a chance to change her mind.

Boothe peeled potatoes. He gave her a brief glance, his mouth set in a tight line. "Aunt Ada's resting."

Jessie sat at the other end of the table, a book before him.

Emma took a few more steps into the room so she could see Jessie better. He glanced at her, his mouth pulled back in an angry frown, his hair mussed as if he'd been pushing it back in frustration. There was no mistaking the glassy look in his eyes.

"Hello," he murmured, his voice croaky as if it took effort to get the word out.

Emma itched to press her palm to his forehead, but she didn't need to touch him to know he ran a fever. She turned to Boothe, undaunted by his glower. "Your son is sick. You need to look after him."

Jessie jumped from his chair. "I want to go home," he wailed and raced for the storeroom where they slept.

Boothe's mouth pulled down into a fierce scowl. "I warned you to stay out of my affairs."

"Strictly speaking, you said not to interfere with your son, but I can't stand by and see him needing medical attention and not getting it. I've seen enough needless suffering for one day." She stopped short of providing any details from the hospital. "Your son has a fever. You should attend to him. I'll finish the potatoes as soon as I've changed."

His eyes darkened with anger, but she met

his gaze boldly, unflinchingly. They looked at each other a long time. She felt as if they dueled with unseen weapons. She would not let him win this silent war. This was not about him proving he didn't need the help of a nurse. This was about a sick little boy needing care. She would not back down and let Jessie or anyone suffer needlessly.

Muttering under his breath about interfering women and controlling nurses, he tossed the paring knife on the table and strode after Jessie.

She called after him. "You might want to sponge him with cool water to lower the fever. And check his cut. If it looks infected, try an old-fashioned remedy like a bread poultice."

She waited to hear Boothe murmur to Jessie. The shrill whine of Jessie's answer sent skitters of alarm up her spine. She hoped home remedies would be enough.

Guessing Boothe might not want to return to the kitchen until she left, and knowing he needed to get water to sponge Jessie and probably prepare a poultice, she headed to her room to change into a warm sweater and skirt.

A wave of discouragement swept over her and she fell to her knees. *God, I can't stand to see so much suffering because of ignorance or stupidity. And it's difficult for me to stand by when I see Jessie needing attention. He's such a sweet boy and is dealing with so much. Heal his cut. Heal their inner hurts.* She didn't question that she meant both Jessie and his father in her last request.

CHAPTER FOUR

Boothe fumed at Emma's insinuation that he didn't know how to care for his son. He might not be as quick to figure out medical needs as she was, but even before her comment, he realized Jessie wasn't just whining because of the move and a new school, though Boothe figured it was more than enough reason to cause the boy to fuss.

He paused outside the storeroom, pulling his angry thoughts into submission before he faced his son.

Jessie lay face down on his bed, sobbing.

Boothe shifted Jessie and perched on the edge of the cot beside him. He rubbed Jessie's back. "I'm sorry things are so hard right now, but I promise they'll get better."

Jessie scrunched away making it plain he cared little for Boothe's promise.

Boothe swept his hand over Jessie's forehead. It did seem warmer than normal. He checked under Jessie's shirt. Again, the boy seemed a bit too warm. "Jessie, I need to check your arm."

Jessie wailed and drew into a ball, pressing a hand to his shoulder as if to prevent Boothe from touching him.

"I have to look at it."

"Leave me alone." Jessie turned his tear-streaked face to Boothe. "I don't want you. I want Auntie Vera."

Boothe's heart stalled as the words pierced his soul. He pulled his hand back and ground his fist into his thigh as if he could force his mind to shift to the pain in his leg. Jessie had no idea how his words hurt, how losing his son's love to Vera and Luke seemed like the final injustice in a list of unexpected, undeserved tragedies.

Ignoring his son's resistance, he turned him to his back. "Do you want to take off your shirt or do you want me to?"

"No."

"I won't hurt you." He unbuttoned the shirt.

"Owwwww."

Boothe ignored the pathetic pleas and sat Jessie up to remove the shirt and lower the top half of the long underwear. He gently touched the arm on either side of the dressing, but he couldn't tell if it seemed unduly warm.

"I have to take off the bandage."

Jessie batted at Boothe's hands. "Don't touch it."

"I have to." He began to unwrap the cloth.

When Jessie realized his protests wouldn't stop Boothe, he settled back and glowered. "You don't care if it hurts."

"Son, I don't want to hurt you. You know that. But if your cut is infected, it has to be treated."

"You don't care."

Boothe's eyes narrowed as he pulled off the pad of cloth and saw the reddened edges of the wound. "I'll have to put a poultice on this." He didn't need Emma to tell him what to do. He knew about poultices because Alyse had put one on his leg when he tore it on barbwire. She'd ignored his protest that it would heal just fine left alone. Silently he thanked her for insisting; otherwise he would not know how to treat their son now.

He tilted his head toward the kitchen and when he determined it was quiet, hurried in and put a small pot of milk on the stove. He had no desire to see Emma or listen to her unwanted advice. Knowing she was a nurse who played with people's lives made his tongue curl with a bitter taste.

As he waited for the milk to heat, he

prepared a thick slice of bread and gathered up clean rags.

He heard Emma's steps on the stairs as he carried his supplies back to the storeroom. The skin on the back of his neck prickled with tension, and he picked up his pace even though he doubted she'd follow him. He put the milk-soaked bread on the wound and wrapped it in place with a length of sheet. According to what he remembered Alyse saying, it had to be left until morning and by then would have drawn out the infection. If not, he would do it again. He would fight for the well-being of his young son. And he would not let someone interfere because they had an education that they thought gave them the right.

Jessie continued to glower at him. "You should have taken me to the doctor like Miss Emma said."

Boothe finished pinning the cloth in place, giving himself time to calm his thoughts. He gently took Jessie's shoulders and squeezed. "Jessie, don't ever think you can turn yourself over to the care of a doctor or nurse and you'll be safe. You must promise me to use your head and do what you need to look after yourself and those you care about."

He waited for Jessie to agree but the boy

only whimpered. Boothe didn't like to press him when he was feeling poorly but this was too important to let go. "Jessie, you have to take care of yourself or let someone who loves you take care of you. Don't trust strangers. You must promise me."

"Okay, I promise."

Boothe wondered if the boy understood, but he would be sure to repeat the warning time and again until Jessie had it firmly in his mind. He did not want to lose his son to a careless nurse or doctor concerned more with their medicines and diagnoses than with the patient. Alyse was not simply a patient. She had been his wife and Jessie's mother.

He sponged Jessie until he seemed less restless. He would have done it without Emma's instructions. He focused on Emma's interference, hoping to keep his fear at bay. It was only a cut. Nothing out of the ordinary for a small boy. He himself had many scars to prove children endured cuts that healed sometimes without so much as being cleaned.

Yet Boothe had overreacted when Jessie ran into the nail on the side of the baggage cart. When he saw the deep tear in Jessie's flesh, he'd roared at the innocent baggage handler. It had taken a long while for his inner turmoil to settle down, for his fears to subside.

Jessie was all he had left. He intended to protect him from danger and interference.

But now he had an infection and Boothe was powerless to fix it.

He felt inadequate trying to be both father and mother. He didn't feel adequate as one parent, let alone trying to be both. But one thing he knew without a flicker of doubt — his son would not ever be subjected to the careless ministrations of a nurse or a doctor.

He let his anger, fear and frustration narrow down to Emma. Just because she was a nurse gave her no right to interfere in his life. Or Jessie's. He'd warn her again to mind her own business. Surely there were enough people at the hospital wanting her help without her having to play nurse at home. Apart from having to sit at the same table for breakfast and supper, he could see no reason for the two of them to spend time together or even speak for that matter.

He sat at the bed until Jessie drifted off to sleep.

When Aunt Ada had admitted she hadn't slept well because of her arthritis, he'd sent her to bed promising to make supper. He returned to the kitchen to fulfill his duty.

Emma stood at the table cleaning up the last of the potato peelings. She glanced up as he entered the room. "How is he?"

"Fine."

"You might want to —"

"Stop. If I want your advice, I'll ask. I want to make myself very clear here." He stood at the doorway, his fists on his hips, and gave her his hardest look. "I don't want your help looking after my child. *I* will see to his needs. Do you hear me?"

She quirked one disbelieving eyebrow. "Of course I hear you. But —"

He shook his head. "No buts. Stay away from Jessie and me. Find someone else to fix if you have such a need."

Her eyes darkened like the approach of night. Her nostrils flared.

He waited, expecting an outburst, or perhaps a hot defense of her abilities.

But she swallowed hard and then blinked twice in rapid succession. "I am not trying to fix anyone, though I wish I had the ability. Believe me, many times a day, I wish I could."

"So long as we understand each other."

"Oh, I think we do, and I don't think keeping out of your way is going to prove too difficult for me."

Her gaze slid past him. He understood

she thought of Jessie.

"Leave Jessie alone."

Before Emma answered, before he could guess what the sudden flash in her eyes meant, Aunt Ada entered the room.

"It's almost time to make supper." She patted a yawn. "I can't believe I slept so long."

"The potatoes are ready to cook." Emma headed for the door, obviously ready and anxious to get away from Boothe. "I'm going to run over to the Douglases."

She left and Boothe turned his attention to supper preparations, slicing pork for frying, pouring applesauce from a jar into a bowl and generally, in his inept way, doing his best to help Aunt Ada.

The meal was almost ready when he heard Emma return. A tightness across his shoulders relaxed. For the past twenty minutes, he wondered if he'd offended her so badly she decided not to come back. Perhaps she would find somewhere else to live. It would prove a relief for him if she did but he knew Aunt Ada needed her boarders, and despite his personal dislike of Emma, she was, no doubt, the sort of boarder Aunt Ada preferred.

Emma slipped into her place at the far

end of the table.

He glanced her way as he placed a bowl mounded with creamy mashed potatoes in the center of the table. He'd done a good job with them, if he did say so himself, though it had taken some direction from Aunt Ada.

He'd expected Emma to be subdued, even a bit sullen after the way he'd spoken to her, and the look of eager anticipation and excitement on her face made him narrow his eyes. Had she found somewhere else to live? Somewhere more welcoming? For Aunt Ada's sake, he hoped not.

"Where's Jessie?" Betty asked.

"He's not feeling well. I've had to sponge him a couple of times to get his fever down." He kept his voice firm to convince one and all he was competent to care for his son without medical interference.

Emma studied him soberly but offered no more advice.

The others murmured sympathy for the little boy.

Loretta, the old dear, offered her own solution. "The boy needs a good dose of salts. That will fix him up in a snap."

Boothe almost laughed at the shock in Emma's face. "I'll keep that in mind."

Though he had no intention of doing such a thing.

Emma's eyes flashed. She opened her mouth, but before she could speak, he shook his head ever so slightly, silently reminding her of his warning. She shut her mouth and fixed him with a deadly look.

He ducked to hide a smile. He almost enjoyed seeing her bristle.

Amidst the general discussion as people dug into the food, complimenting both he and Aunt Ada, Boothe stole several glances at Emma. Her anger at him had disappeared as quickly as it came, replaced with the same eagerness she'd had when she returned. He wondered what sparked the flashing light in her eyes and again hoped she wouldn't decide to move out.

The food disappeared quickly. He helped Aunt Ada serve the butterscotch pudding she'd made earlier in the day. As everyone enjoyed the dessert, Emma leaned forward.

"Listen everyone," she began.

Boothe waited for the announcement.

"I went to visit Pastor and Mrs. Douglas this afternoon. You all know how difficult things have been for them this year with Pastor Douglas recovering from a stroke."

Boothe listened to the murmurs of acknowledgment. Was she going to move in with them?

"They always make gifts for each child at the Christmas concert." Emma edged forward and glanced around the table, her expression eager as she looked at each one until her gaze settled on Boothe. Then her eyes grew wary.

Then she skipped past him and continued. "With all they've had to deal with, they haven't got the gifts made. Mrs. Douglas was fretting about how to get thirty or forty gifts done in time. I thought we could do something to help. What do you think?"

There was silence for a moment while everyone digested her request. For his part, Boothe had to work hard to keep from exhaling his relief over her announcement. Her excitement was only about taking over a project and getting them all involved.

Betty spoke first. "Forty gifts? How on earth did they ever do it themselves?"

Emma nodded. "I know. I wondered the same."

"What sort of things do they normally make?" Sarah asked.

"Generally, wooden toys for the boys, dolls for the girls. and Mrs. Douglas said they also like to make sure every child gets a pair of mittens."

"Goodness," Ed said. "Forty gifts."

"I thought if we worked in the evenings, making it a group project instead of reading our book . . . Just until this is done," Emma added as the others protested. "Pastor Douglas sent the pattern for trucks and trains. He said if anyone can carve, you could make airplanes with little propellers that turn. Wait, I'll show you." She hurried out to the hall and returned with a large wooden box that she put on the floor by her chair. She pulled out pieces of wood. "He even got a few cut before his stroke. They only need to be sanded and painted." She finally sat back, quiet, waiting for the others to respond.

"Forty toys," Ed said again.

Loretta clapped her hands. "Well, of course the children must have their gifts. I can certainly knit mittens."

"I'll knit some, too," Aunt Ada said.

"I can sew things," Sarah added.

"Thank you." Emma turned to Ed and Don. "Can you help with the wooden toys?"

"Forty gifts?" Ed said.

Betty snapped her fingers in his face. "Ed, get over it. Say you'll help. I'm going to."

Everyone laughed at how quickly Ed agreed. Don added his promise to help.

Emma slid her glance over Boothe. "Good." She rubbed her hands together.

"As soon as the kitchen is cleaned, let's get started. We have a lot to do."

Boothe stared at her. Was he invisible? Wasn't he allowed to be part of this? His eyes narrowed. Did she think he'd refuse simply because it was her idea? Or because she'd be there? Admittedly, a part of him rebelled at the idea of working with her. But what was he supposed to do? Sit by idly while everyone else made gifts for the children? And he was the only one with a child of his own. It simply wasn't right. "I'll help, too."

Emma gazed in his direction. "That's very generous of you." Her words sounded like she'd dragged them from the icebox.

"You're welcome. I'm proud to do my part." Not giving her a chance to respond, he grabbed a handful of plates and strode to the kitchen.

As he washed dishes, having appointed himself chief cook and bottle washer, his thoughts mocked him. *Avoid her. You only have to see her at supper and breakfast. Stay away from her and her interfering ways. And the first time something comes up where you don't have to be in the same room, jump right in and volunteer.* Oh yes. He certainly made a wise move there.

The evening barely got underway before

he knew he'd made a mistake. Emma took control of the proceedings in such a high-handed way that he bit his tongue to keep from protesting. Only Aunt Ada and Loretta escaped her control as they retired to the front room, sorted through yarn and started on the mittens.

Emma put out fabric on the table, some already cut into rag doll shapes, and gave Betty and Sarah each a job. She ordered Ed and Don to the corner of the room. "We don't want to mess up Ada's kitchen any more than necessary." Ed and Don obeyed like young boys and immediately began sanding pieces. She looked at Boothe, shrugged and left him to decide what he wanted to do.

He didn't want to be ordered about, but he also didn't want to be ignored as if she didn't care to acknowledge his presence — maybe even his existence. "I'm going to try my hand at carving a propeller." He grabbed a chair and joined Ed and Don in the corner.

As they worked, they talked. And Boothe listened.

"Any news from Kody and Charlotte?" asked Betty.

Boothe learned that Kody was the Douglas's son and he and his wife owned a ranch in the hills.

"I haven't seen them in a while," Emma said. "I might have to go out there on my day off."

At the lonesome tone in her voice, Boothe glanced her way. Did nurses feel the same emotions as others? Somehow he expected they functioned like machines — bossy machines — with no concern about how people felt. That she'd reveal ordinary emotions surprised him.

Two hours later, she stood. "That's enough for tonight." She looked at the doll Sarah was working on. "This is sweet." Boothe glanced over. Sarah had embroidered a lifelike face.

Betty threw down the doll she worked on. "Mine looks stupid. It has button eyes."

Emma retrieved it. "This is fine. And your sewing is so strong. It will stand up to a lot of loving. Why don't you, Sarah, do the faces and you, Betty, stitch them together? That way you both get to do what you do best."

Betty puckered her mouth. "You aren't just trying to butter me up?"

Emma laughed. "I'm being practical."

Ed chuckled. "Betty, you know Emma doesn't say things she doesn't mean. Hey, look at my truck. Vroom, vroom."

Everyone laughed as he played with the wooden automobile he'd sanded to satin smoothness.

Don exhibited his project — train wheels. "Now show us what you did," he said to Boothe.

Reluctantly, Boothe held out the propeller he worked on. "When I'm done, it should spin freely."

"We accomplished a lot." Emma gathered together the sewing. Don put the wooden pieces into the box Pastor Douglas sent.

Boothe assessed the toys. He tallied the items already cut out and did a quick estimate. Once the shapes were cut out, the work went quickly and could be done in the evenings. However, there needed to be a lot more pieces cut.

Emma wiped the table. Boothe grabbed the broom as she reached for it and swept the floor.

She paused at the box of wood and looked thoughtful. "We need to find someone to cut out more shapes for us."

The others had left the room so Boothe felt compelled to answer. "I'm sure you'll think of something."

"You sound disapproving. Why?"

He concentrated on sweeping up the wood dust. He hadn't meant to sound like a man with a mouthful of vinegar.

"Do you think you can protect yourself by pushing everyone away? Aren't you afraid you'll get lonely?"

Her words slammed against his heart. Boothe stopped sweeping. He closed his eyes and squeezed the broom handle so hard that he felt a sliver stab his palm. No, he wasn't lonely.

Jessie cried out. Boothe dropped the broom and headed for their room. He'd checked Jessie several times throughout the evening and figured the temperature remained down. He resisted the temptation to take the poultice off and look underneath. Only Alyse's words stopped him. She'd laughed at him when he tried to pull the poultice off his leg. "Stop trying to rush things. Let it do its work."

As he soothed Jessie from his nightmare, relieved his son seemed only normally warm from sleep, Boothe felt a great tear in his heart. He would endure loneliness to protect Jessie. He heard Emma still tidying. For a moment, he considered returning to the kitchen and her company. Instead, he stared out the window in to the dark, feeling the gloom settle into his soul.

CHAPTER FIVE

Emma hurried into the kitchen and laid out the yard goods she'd purchased at the store. If she cut out several dolls, the work would go faster. As Ed said, forty gifts was a lot. As she pinned the pattern pieces, Jessie bounced into the room singing a tuneless song. Boothe had assured everyone over breakfast that his son had slept well, but he'd let him stay home from school.

Emma smiled at Jessie. His eyes were bright and clear, his color good and he seemed about to erupt with pent-up energy. His eager smile made her want to hug him. "You must be feeling better."

Jessie stopped jumping about and pulled his face into a dark frown. "My arm sure hurts a lot. I don't think I'll be able to go to school. Won't be able to write, you know."

Emma laughed at his sudden change in demeanor. Jessie's recovery appeared to depend on being able to stay home. To test her theory, she said, "No more school today."

Immediately Jessie went from a lifeless wooden puppet to an animated little boy. "What did you do today?"

What a fun child. She loved children who showed a little spark. "I went to work." She paused, wondering how much of Boothe's anger toward medicine Jessie absorbed. "At the hospital, remember?"

"My daddy says I must never go to a hospital."

"Sometimes it's the best place to be."

Jessie squinted at her. "My daddy says you have to take care of yourself or let someone who loves you do it."

Emma fought hard to mind her own business. She'd promised herself to do her best to get along with Boothe. Teaching his child the benefits of modern medicine would not accomplish that goal. She wouldn't go so far as to directly go against his wishes but perhaps she could plant a little seed of reason. "Sometimes only a doctor can help you." She decided to change the subject before it went any further. "Where's your daddy?"

"He's downstairs making something. I'm not 'lowed to go down there." Jessie sighed long, communicating how sad it made him to have to obey his father's orders.

"And Aunt Ada?" Emma continued to cut out the fabric.

"She went upstairs to check on Miss Loretta. Whatcha doing?"

Emma paused. Jessie would be one of the children receiving a gift. Should he see them before it was time? She glanced at the box holding the wooden cars and trains. Someone had covered it with a blanket. "We're making rag dolls." She guessed he wouldn't care about the girls' gifts.

"Dolls? Ech!"

Emma laughed. "Do you want one?"

Jessie scooted backward. "I'm no girl."

Emma pretended to give him lots of study. Again, she noticed his fine clothes. From what Aunt Ada said, she gathered Boothe struggled to care for his son. "No work and trying to be both mother and father. It's been rough," she'd said. And yet the sweater and trousers looked expensive. Jessie regarded her with a wide-eyed expression. Something about this child appealed to her at a deep level.

She recognized her denied maternal instinct. She'd love a child of her own with the same spunk, the same golden glow, the same —

God, I again give You my desires. I want

78

only to do what is right. I know You have set before me a responsibility, and I will not shirk it or regret it.

She waited a moment for peace and contentment to return.

"I ain't no girl," Jessie repeated.

"I'm *not* a girl," she corrected. "And I can plainly see you're a big strong boy."

He pushed his chest out and lifted his chin.

Behind him the basement door clicked and he spun around. "Daddy, are you done now?"

Boothe stepped into the room, carrying a box. "For now." He saw Emma at the table and his eyes narrowed. "What are you doing, Jessie?"

"Me and Miss Emma were talking."

Emma's cheeks burned with guilt. She kept her head down, afraid to meet Boothe's gaze as she waited for Jessie to tell his father about their discussion over hospitals.

"She said I could have a doll." Jessie's comment dripped with disgust.

Boothe chuckled, pulling Emma's gaze from her work. His eyes seemed softer, like the first gentle light of morning. He held her gaze for a heartbeat and then another. Her heart felt as if it stopped beating as something passed between them, something fragile, tenuous, unfamiliar and slightly frightening.

"I told her I'm not a girl." Jessie's voice sliced through the moment.

Boothe grinned at his son.

Emma's blood rushed to her limbs with a jolt. She grabbed the edge of the table as her legs shook. How could she explain what had just happened? For one brief moment, it seemed as if they'd both forgotten their differences and —

What? She grabbed the scissors and resumed cutting.

They only acknowledged shared amusement over Jessie's disgust. Nothing more.

"Jessie, would you go to the bedroom and find my knife? I think I dropped it on the floor this morning."

As soon as Jessie ran from the room, Boothe crossed the floor. Emma told herself she wasn't any more aware of him then she'd been this morning, or last night. He was a rude, backward man who relegated her profession to something akin to a snake oil salesman. She couldn't believe she gave him more than a passing glance the first time she saw him.

But as he passed, her cheeks burned and she shifted sideways to avoid looking at him.

"Lift the blanket off this box for me,

would you?"

She jumped as if he'd snuck up on her and shouted *boo!* The scissors clattered across the table. She spun around. He stood beside the box of wood and waited, his expression watchful. She took a deep breath and prayed he hadn't noticed her foolish reaction.

"The blanket?" He nodded toward the box.

She snatched it off and clutched it to her chest.

He dumped the contents of the box into the larger one on the floor.

Emma gaped. "You've cut out more trucks and trains."

"I had nothing else to do. I haven't found a job yet. And Aunt Ada doesn't need help for more than a few hours a day."

She stared at him. "Boothe Wallace, you surprise me."

"How so?"

"I —" It didn't sound very nice to say she expected him to criticize her project. "You —" Saying he didn't seem the kind to help didn't sound any better. "You just do."

He considered her long enough to make her squirm, then reached for the blanket. As his fingers brushed the back of her hand, she jerked back a step.

"I'm assuming Jessie will be one of the children receiving a gift. The least I can do is help." He rubbed his hands together as Jessie returned waving the knife.

"Found it under the bed."

"Good job. Now let's get your things ready for school tomorrow."

The two of them left the room, Jessie protesting loudly. "My arm hurts. My stomach aches."

"You'll be fine."

"No, I won't."

Emma grabbed the scissors and returned to cutting out rag dolls, pushing her thoughts firmly back in place. Boothe made it clear as glass what he thought of her being a nurse. She might as well expect the moon to land at her feet as to think he might show a speck of interest in her.

Emma stood before the front door and took a deep breath. Thankfully she'd been too busy all day to dwell on how silly she'd acted yesterday. For the most part, she'd been able to pretend her heart hadn't given a quick little kick against her ribs every time she glanced at Boothe. But standing on the step, her cheeks burned to think how she'd reacted to his soft smile. She feared her eyes revealed a glimpse of her dreams for love and family.

Lord, help me be sensible. Give me Your peace. She waited a moment then stepped inside.

She heard Jessie and Boothe talking in the kitchen. She hurried up the stairs to change, ignoring the way her heart clamored for a glimpse of the pair. She took her time pulling off her uniform and selecting the outfit she wanted. Then she brushed back the strands of hair that had fallen from her bun.

She was a nurse. He hated nurses. It was as simple as that.

Yes, an inner voice argued, apart from that, he's a good man, he loves his son and —

Enough of that. You're a practical person, Emma Spencer. There is no room in your life for such things, even if Boothe liked you, which he most certainly does not.

Her responsibilities could not be changed. And she got a great deal of joy out of nursing. She'd had the satisfaction of seeing that very sick young man improve before she left the hospital. He stood a fair chance of a complete recovery. Tucking her practical acceptance about her, she headed down the stairs.

Boothe bent over Jessie, who was seated at the table, running his finger along a page.

"What's this word?"

Emma sucked in a deep breath at the sight of the pair.

"Daddy, I can't read." Jessie sounded ready to cry.

"No one can at first. But you already know this word."

"I forget." Jessie practically choked on a sob.

Boothe's lips grew tight. Emma feared the man would be angry, disappointed with his son, but when he looked up, she saw he wasn't angry but hurting for his son's frustration. "It's okay, Jessie," he said. "I'll help you." He squeezed his son's shoulders and kissed the top of his head.

Swallowing hard at the sudden emotion clogging her throat, Emma glanced away. All her life she'd had a dream — two actually. She'd dreamed of being a nurse and helping others get better. She had always planned to do that for a time before she pursued her second dream — a man who loved her and showed her tender feelings. She knew her father loved her, but he didn't show it in touches or words. He only showed it in acknowledging her successes and commenting on her accomplishments. Secretly, she longed for more.

She would get even less if he knew —

She stopped herself from following that trail.

With a gentle touch, a kiss, Boothe assured Jessie of his love even when he couldn't do a task. Had he shown the same love to his wife?

She forced her thoughts in a safer direction. She would never be able to experience her second dream. Speaking cheerfully, she said, "Hello, everyone," and went to Ada's side where she stirred a simmering pot of soup. "Anything I can do to help?"

She would not allow herself to look at Boothe.

Jessie scrambled from the chair and rushed to her side. "Daddy made me go to school today."

"Yes, I heard." She bent to his level. "How did it go?"

He shrugged. "I've had better days."

She hid a smile and glanced at Boothe. A grin tugged at his mouth, making it impossible for Emma to pretend indifference. Tearing her gaze away, she turned back to Jessie. "I'm sure it will get better."

He looked unconvinced.

"What was the best thing about your day?"

He thought for a moment then brightened. "At recess we practiced throwing sticks and I threw mine the farthest. Even

85

farther than some of the big boys." His chest expanded. "They said I could play ball with them." His shoulders caved in. "But we had to go inside and we didn't play ball at all."

Emma ruffled his hair, liking its fine texture. "I'm sure you'll get a chance. They aren't likely to forget you were the best thrower, now are they?"

He grinned. "Uncle Luke taught me how to throw good."

Emma glanced toward Boothe again, wanting to share her pleasure in Jessie's pride, but instead of smiling, he scowled, his expression dark, almost angry. When he saw she watched him, he turned his back. Why should he get upset at the mention of an uncle?

Jessie tugged at her hand. "I've forgotten how to read." He pulled her toward the table and showed her his reader. "I could before we moved."

She stood beside him, aching to pull him close and assure him things would get better. "I wouldn't worry too much. I remember one summer I forgot some real easy words like 'the' and 'how.' And I was in fourth grade. It soon came back." She also remembered how afraid she'd been her father would find out and be unhappy with her.

"I guess so."

"I heard your daddy say he'd help you."

Jessie turned the book round and round studying it from each direction. Suddenly he sat up. "Maybe you can help me, too."

Emma couldn't answer. Her chest felt tight. A rush of longing flooded over her as she acknowledged her impossible dreams — a man to love her and show that love in concrete ways, a man like Boothe, a child to pour her love over, and a child like Jessie. She forced herself to take a deep breath, chasing away her foolish thoughts. "I'd like to, if your father doesn't mind." She finally dared raise her gaze to Boothe, uncertain what to expect. Would he resent her interference or welcome her help? He'd made it clear he didn't want her medical advice. Would this be any different?

He stared at his son, a bleak look on his face.

Emma lowered her gaze back to Jessie's reader, unable to bear the pain she saw in Boothe's eyes, wishing she could ease it.

Mumbling something about needing to check the furnace, Boothe strode from the room.

Jessie watched every step that took his father out of sight. He gave a shaky sigh. "Where is Daddy going?"

"To the basement," Emma said. "He'll be back in a minute."

"He's been up and down at least a dozen times," Ada added. "Found a box of clothes I said he could have. I can't even remember who left them. He's fixed a leaky pipe and stopped a hole where the mice were getting in." She chuckled. "I'm liking the idea of him living here more and more."

"I don't want to live here," Jessie whispered. "I want to go home."

Ada limped over and sat across from him. She took his hands between her own. "Jessie, we're family. My house is your house."

"But I want my Auntie Vera."

Ada opened her arms and Jessie scrambled from the chair. Sobbing, he threw himself into her embrace. "I miss my auntie. Why did we have to go away?"

"There, there, child." Ada's eyes filled with tears. "You'll be safe here."

Safe from what? Emma wondered at Ada's choice of words.

Boothe rattled up the stairs. Jessie flew into his arms. "I don't want to stay here. I want to go home. Why can't I?"

Boothe hugged the boy tight.

Emma's eyes burned with tears she would not allow to fall. Everything in her called to hold Jessie, rock him and soothe away his fears. But to him, she was only a stranger in an unfamiliar house.

She spun around and headed for the closet under the stairs where Ada stored books and games. She found the one she noticed weeks ago. A story of Joseph written for children. She plucked it from the shelf and returned to the kitchen.

Boothe stood over the stove. She sensed tension in his stiff posture. Again she wished she could do something to ease his pain. Medicine relieved physical pain, but time seemed the only cure for emotional pain.

She turned to Jessie. "I have a story here about a boy whose mother died and he had to leave home even though he didn't want to."

Jessie's eyes grew round. "What did he do?"

"Do you want me to read it?"

He nodded eagerly.

Emma glanced at Boothe, silently seeking his permission.

His eyes dark, his expression bleak, he nodded.

She pulled a chair to Jessie's side, put the book on the table in front of him and read how Joseph was sold to slave traders and taken far away from his father and home.

Jessie put his hand on the book before she

turned the page. "That was really mean, wasn't it?"

Emma agreed. "But that wasn't the end of the story because, you see, God had a plan for Joseph."

She turned the page and read, " 'But the Lord was with Joseph.' You see, no matter what people did to Joseph, they couldn't stop God's plan." She read the quick summary that took Joseph from Potiphar to prison to the Pharaoh's throne. And then the final scene with his brothers. "Listen to what Joseph says, 'You thought to do me evil but God meant it for good to save His people.' "

Jessie looked thoughtful. "What does that mean?"

"It means God uses everything for our good and the good of others."

Jessie looked surprised and then pleased. He bounced off the chair and raced to Boothe's side. "Did you hear that, Daddy? God will make everything turn out good."

"I guess that's right." He lifted his gaze to Emma, his eyes full of dark mystery she couldn't interpret. She turned away first, uncomfortable with his intense look.

Thankfully, Ada spoke and broke the tension. "Emma, how thoughtful of you."

Boothe cleared his throat. "Yes, thank you."

Just then, the other boarders trooped in. A short time later, supper was served. Afterward, as Boothe supervised the cleanup, Jessie edged close to Emma, his reader clutched to his chest.

" 'Member you said you'd help me?"

Emma bent over to look directly into Jessie's blue eyes. "Did you ask your daddy if it's okay?"

He turned toward Boothe. "Daddy?"

Boothe, his hands submerged in water as he washed the dishes, glanced over his shoulder. "If Miss Emma doesn't mind."

Emma didn't mind a bit and followed Jessie to the table. He placed the reader between them and smoothed the pages open. "It isn't as good as the story you read me." His voice crackled as he bent over the page.

Emma sensed he was tense because he couldn't remember how to read, so she talked about the pictures in the book, laughing at the expression on Dick's face.

"That's Dick's name." Jessie said, his voice round with excitement. "I remember that." He bent over the page, struggled to form the words in his mind. *"See Dick. See Dick run."*

Emma clapped. "I knew you'd remember."

Jessie grinned so widely that his eyes squeezed shut.

Boothe paused at the table. "That was great, son. You did well. Thank Miss Emma for helping you." Boothe's gray eyes warmed with what she took for approval.

"Thank you, Miss Emma," Jessie said.

Emma forced her gaze to Jessie. "You're most welcome." She couldn't bring herself to look at Boothe again, afraid her face would reveal how much she reveled in his appreciation.

Life settled into a routine. After supper, when Jessie had gone to bed, the boarders worked on the Christmas toys. Every day Sarah brought home a little dress she'd made for the dolls and fancy material to make others. Boothe carved half a dozen propellers and affixed them to wooden airplanes. Daily, the pile of toys grew larger.

Emma smiled as she entered the house. They all seemed to enjoy themselves as they worked together. As Boothe relaxed around them, she discovered he was an amusing storyteller.

Recalling his story last night, she laughed softly.

"I found work helping haul logs out of the

woods. The man I worked for had this knothead of a horse. It seemed to me the horse went out of his way to complicate matters so he could rest while we tried to fix things." He chuckled.

Emma noticed his expression grew gentle, making him look younger. He had a strong chin and a wide smile when he forgot his troubles. She'd wrenched her thoughts back to the rag doll she stitched together.

Boothe continued his story. "Old Barney had a knack for getting stuck on a stump. Then he couldn't seem to remember how to back up or turn around. I tell you, I've never seen a horse act so stupid when he was just plain smarter than either of us wanted to admit." He laughed, his voice deep with amusement. "One time he got himself all tangled up in the traces. Mr. MacLeod told Old Barney the only reason he was still standing was because he hadn't brought a gun. MacLeod sweated and grumbled and Old Barney played dumb. We finally got him straightened round and MacLeod was so angry that he shook his fist in Barney's face and threatened to knock him cold. Wouldn't you know it? Old Barney pretended MacLeod frightened him and took off like a shot, knocking MacLeod off his feet. The horse stopped a few yards away and put on a great show of being scared half to death. I laughed so hard I had to lean against a tree. MacLeod picked himself up, grabbed a hunk of tree and brandished it. I wasn't sure who he wanted to hit most — me or Old Barney."

Emma's smile deepened. Boothe seemed the kind of man who had been able to find humor in most situations. She wondered if he still had the ability.

It was a good thing she had to go to work each day. Too much time spent in his company might make it hard for her to remember her responsibilities. Once Emma was inside, she went for the mail Ada always left on the tiny table in the hall. Emma shuffled through the letters and found one from home. She opened it and skimmed the two tightly written pages. Mom wrote almost every week — always including a detailed weather report. "Wind on Monday. More wind on Tuesday and falling temperatures. It was so cold we couldn't get more than two feet from the stove. Even staying close, we baked on one side and froze on the other. Wednesday, it snowed a little. Not really snow though. Just hard little pellets." Emma skipped the rest of the weather news, looking for Sid's name. She found it near the bottom of the second page. "Sid misses you. Says to tell you to come home soon."

Emma read the rest of the letter, then returned it to the envelope. She missed her brother. She'd make plans to visit in the near future.

But would she ever see Sid without experiencing as much pain and regret as she did pleasure?

CHAPTER SIX

Boothe hurried toward the boardinghouse. He'd planned to be home by the time Jessie got back from school but Mr. White at the garage had been interested in Boothe's ability to tinker with engines. He'd taken Boothe into the shop and asked him to look at a 1928 Dodge. Boothe had breathed deeply, contentedly, of the smell of grease and oil, then bent over and poked around the engine. He made a few adjustments then cranked over the motor. He listened, adjusted the choke and nodded. "Sounds good."

Mr. White handed Boothe a rag to wipe his hands on. "Does indeed. You say you're looking for a job?"

"Could use some work all right."

"Then show up here tomorrow morning around eight."

Boothe hesitated.

"There a problem?"

"Got me a boy with no mother. I'd like to see him to school before I come in." Jessie whined and fussed if Boothe wasn't close by. Boothe couldn't be there every waking moment but neither could he expect Aunt Ada to get the resisting child off to school.

"It's gotta be tough for you both." Mr. White shoved out a meaty, grease-stained hand. "Nine will be fine. Nothing that can't wait until then."

Boothe paused on the step of Aunt Ada's house. He wasn't looking forward to Jessie's complaining about Boothe's absence. He didn't know how he'd deal with it day after day now that he had a job. But having a steady income was essential in order to keep Jessie.

He stepped inside and stood still. He'd expected whining but heard Jessie laughing. Emma's voice joined. Surprised and curious, he dropped his cap on a hook and edged toward the kitchen door.

The pair sat on the floor facing each other, their attention on something between them. He strained forward trying to glimpse what it was without alerting them to his presence. Seeing Jessie playing happily, laughing and relaxed even though Boothe was absent, gave him a queer twist of pleasure and relief. He'd almost forgotten what it was like to come home to such a scene.

"My turn," Emma said, leaning forward to scoop something toward her — dominoes. She lined them up like soldiers in a long squiggly row. "Now."

Jessie tipped the first one and laughed as the row fell in a chain reaction. He reached out to pull them close. "My turn." He saw Boothe and jumped to his feet. "We're playing knock 'em down dominoes. It's fun." He grabbed Boothe's hand. "Come and play with us."

Emma pulled her feet beneath her and began to stand. Jessie caught her shoulder. "You have to play, too."

Boothe sensed her reluctance and wondered if she objected to being in his presence. He'd given her plenty of reason. He'd warned her repeatedly to stay away from him and his son. Nevertheless, he was glad she hadn't taken him literally. She'd soothed Jessie's fears by sharing the Joseph story. Jessie had repeated it many times to him, finding comfort in the words, "God will make everything turn out for good."

"What are the rules?" he asked.

"See who can make the longest chain fall down," Jessie said.

Emma settled back to the floor. "See how much fun we can have," she murmured.

Fun. When was the last time he'd done something just for fun? It seems he'd forgotten how.

"You go first," Jessie said, pushing the dominoes toward Boothe.

"Put your foot out and hold still. I'm going to build a fence around it." He set up the dominoes, gauging how far apart to place them in order for them to still tip each other. Jessie giggled as Boothe placed one close to his ankle.

"There." Boothe sat back and pulled his knees up to lean on. "Don't move."

Jessie looked surprised at his order. And then he realized Boothe teased him and chuckling, touched the first domino in the line. He broke into peals of laughter and fell sideways to the floor as the chain snaked around his foot.

Joy, uncommon and unfamiliar, unfolded at Jessie's pure enjoyment of the moment and somewhere, deep inside Boothe's heart, a crack mended. Boothe grinned wide enough to stretch his cheeks. And then he chortled. He chuckled. He laughed until his sides hurt.

Emma's eyes widened with what he could only assume was surprise. Was it that strange for him to enjoy himself? Her surprise faded, replaced with a warm glow, and she chuckled softly.

His laughter abated, though he couldn't stop smiling, and he studied her. He'd never noticed how thick her hair was, the color of ripe straw. Strands hung loose from her bun, trailing down her back almost to her waist.

She blinked and jumped up.

He sobered. He'd been staring rudely. He jerked to his feet. "Pick up the dominoes, Jessie, and put them away." He tried to sort his scrambled thoughts. "Emma —" He didn't want to say he was sorry. He wouldn't take back one fraction of the last couple minutes — laughing with Jessie, sharing the moment with Emma, enjoying a short time in which he forgot his troubles. "I've never thanked you properly for reading Jessie the story of Joseph. He got a great deal of comfort from it."

She nodded and smiled, her eyes following Jessie as he put the game away in the cupboard under the stairs. "I'm glad." She shifted her gaze to Boothe and he felt her growing intensity. "It's a good reminder for us all."

His heart beat hard in his chest. He wanted to believe as he used to — simple, unquestioning, untried belief in God's goodness, in His promise to turn everything into something good. "How does the murder of one's wife turn out for good?"

She reached out, her expression filled with pain.

Shrugging away from her hand, he walked out of the room. He didn't want to hear empty platitudes. What did she know about dealing with such useless, painful loss?

"I don't want to go to school," Jessie said, as he and Boothe walked in that direction. Every day it was the same but his protests grew less demanding; now mere words he repeated out of habit.

"Looks like it might snow today."

Jessie looked into the sky with sudden interest. "Do I have to go to school if it snows?"

"Unless we have a storm, yes."

"I hope it storms."

"Storms can be nasty, you know."

"I could stay home and play games with you and Emma."

"You'd like that, would you?" He and Emma had played games several times with Jessie. Old Maid, Snap and Go Fish. But Jessie's favorite remained dominoes. Boothe also held a special regard for the game. It had signaled a change in his relationship with Jessie.

Jessie let out a long-suffering sigh. "I wish

you got home earlier so we could play more games."

"Me, too." By the time he returned from his job, he felt duty bound to help Aunt Ada with supper, though often Emma had done much of it. "How about after supper tonight we play whatever game you want?"

"Goodie." Once they reached the schoolyard, Jessie allowed Boothe to hug him, then ran to join the other children.

Later, his day at the garage finished, Boothe hurried home. He looked forward to spending some time with his son. He hoped Emma would join them. He slowed. What did it matter if she did or not? She was, he reminded himself, a nurse. He had no use for anyone involved in the medical profession. But his silent protests got all tangled up with mental pictures of her playing with Jessie, sharing a laugh with him over his son's enthusiasm.

He shook his head, trying to clear his thoughts but succeeded only in giving himself a headache.

He rushed into the house with unusual haste, tossed his cap to the hook and shed his coat so fast the arms turned inside out. A murmur came from the kitchen and he hurried in that direction.

Jessie sat at the table making a puzzle Aunt Ada had given him. His aunt sat before a basin of carrots, peeling them and slicing them into a pot. He glanced around. There was no one else in the room.

"Hello," he said, a little louder than necessary. In the back of his mind, where he didn't have to admit it to himself, he hoped to alert anyone who might be elsewhere in the house.

Jessie bounced from the chair and rushed to Boothe's side. "Miss Emma can't come home." He tugged Boothe's hand.

"Oh?" Curiosity mingled with disappointment. He turned to Aunt Ada, silently seeking an explanation.

"Didn't you hear about the accident?" she asked.

Accident? Alarm roared through his veins. Emma? And she was at the hospital? His first thought was to rush out the door and snatch her from that place. Away from doctors and nurses who cared only about their medicines. He shook his head. "I've had my head buried under the hood of a truck all day."

"Surprising," his aunt said. "I thought everyone in town knew."

"I heard at school," Jessie said. "Even though the teacher warned the big kids they shouldn't talk about it in front of the little ones." He puffed out his cheeks. "I'm not a little kid."

"What happened?" Boothe barely managed to squeeze out the words.

"A car was hit by the train south of here. A whole family in the car was injured. I heard there were three children besides the parents." Aunt Ada tsked. "It's a miracle they —" She glanced at Jessie and paused. "That they survived."

"Miss Emma has to help," Jessie said.

"Someone brought us a message," Aunt Ada explained. "I don't know when she'll be home."

Relief warred with anger. Emma wasn't at the mercy of someone who considered themself a miracle healer. No. She was one of *those* people. A bitter taste burned the back of his throat. How could he have almost ignored the fact she was a nurse just because she made him laugh? Made Jessie laugh. Gave him looks that turned all his firm determinations into warm butter. How could he have encouraged her friendship with Jessie?

"Daddy?" Jessie jerked Boothe's hand. "Are you sad?"

"I need coffee," Boothe mumbled, pulling away from his son to pour a cupful from the pot on the back of the stove. The brew tasted like the dregs from breakfast, but he forced himself to swallow one mouthful after another.

Jessie watched, his eyes round.

Boothe turned and met Aunt Ada's curious look. No doubt they found his sudden need of old coffee as strange as his reaction. "It's been a long day." He pulled out a chair and sat down.

"She promised to play dominoes with me." Jessie sounded like he'd lost his best friend.

"I'll play with you."

"You aren't as much fun."

Boothe swallowed another mouthful of coffee as bitter memories assaulted him. Alyse was gone because of a nurse and doctor who insisted they knew more than Boothe. He'd never be able to completely shut from his mind the horrible pictures of her last hours.

He'd almost lost Jessie because he'd blindly trusted someone. And yet he'd been lulled into letting Jessie grow fond of Emma. "We'll play something else then."

"Okay."

Boothe ignored the heaviness in his chest rendering his lungs inadequate and forced a smile to his mouth. He turned to his aunt.

"What can I do to help?"

Aunt Ada listed some chores.

Boothe dove into them hoping work would banish thoughts of Emma from his head. But when they sat down to eat, Emma's empty spot at the table mocked his efforts at dismissing her. He forced his attention to his anger at the medical profession. He focused on remembering Emma in her uniform. He filled his memory with bitter thoughts of Alyse's death.

The conversation centered on the accident.

"I wonder how they're doing," Betty said. "I heard the little girl was hurt the worst."

Aunt Ada put down her fork. "Let's pray for them and for Emma. We all know how broken she'll be if they don't pull through."

Boothe bowed his head last. He wanted to believe their prayers held some value, but God certainly hadn't listened to Boothe's desperate pleas for Alyse. But perhaps He listened to the prayers of others. Aunt Ada prayed aloud. The others murmured, "Amen." For himself, he felt only doubt and disbelief, silently drowning the things he'd once believed with such blind faith.

He washed dishes, tended the furnace and played a short-lived game of Old Maid with Jessie, who said he preferred to do his puzzle. Later, he tucked his son into bed, listened to his prayers and helped work on the Christmas toys, silently listening to the others talk about the accident. All the time he seemed to be waiting, listening for something.

The others finished their work and wandered off to bed. The house creaked as it settled into the cold night.

Boothe sat at the table. He couldn't even say what it was he waited for. He only knew something kept his mind on edge. The night ticked away. He drummed his fingers on the table.

Hinges squeaked and he leaped to his feet so fast the chair tipped. He righted it then strode to the hall.

Emma leaned against the front door, her eyes closed.

"You look tired."

She didn't bother to open her eyes. "I am."

"Do you want tea or something to eat?"

She sighed and pushed herself upright. "Tea might be good." She shrugged out of her cape and draped it over the banister. There were blood spatters on her apron.

Boothe tried not to think what it represented — injury, pain, death. He hurried to the stove and pulled the kettle to a hot spot.

Emma sank wearily to a chair, propped

her elbows on the table and leaned heavily into her palms. "It's been a long day."

Boothe poured boiling water over the tea leaves without answering.

"Thank God they are all going to be all right, though it was touch and go for the youngest girl."

Boothe put two teacups on the table, set out cream and sugar and added a plate of Aunt Ada's raisin cookies. So they all pulled through. Because of prayer? If so, why did God grant *this* prayer and deny another? Didn't Boothe need a wife and Jessie a mother as much as this family needed each other?

"Thank you." Emma gave him a weak smile. He sensed it took almost more energy than she had left.

"Have some cookies." He shoved the plate toward her.

At first she looked at them with little interest, then took one as if it required too much effort to refuse.

Boothe watched her swallow tea and nibble at the cookie. And waited for what he still didn't know.

"It was a miracle any of them survived," Emma said. "As we worked over them, I prayed harder than I've ever prayed before."

"Maybe it was plain good luck or —" He

wanted to think God had no hand in it, but if he took God out of the picture, he didn't know what or who else to give credit to.

"You don't really believe that, do you?"

He turned his teacup round and round. "Makes as much sense as believing prayer makes a difference."

"Doesn't make any sense at all."

He shoved the teacup away and stared at her. Despite her weariness, fire flashed through her eyes. She believed wholeheartedly. He wished he could. "What use are prayers if some are answered and others are ignored or denied?"

Her expression softened. "You're talking about yourself, aren't you? About losing your wife?" She didn't give him a chance to deny it. "Was she a Christian?"

He nodded.

"Then she's gone to heaven. Perhaps she's escaped something in the future that would be horrible."

He snorted. "So if someone dies, it's for their good? That doesn't make any sense. How is Alyse's death good for Jessie?"

She sighed wearily. "Boothe, I honestly don't know the answer to why some people die early, others suffer a long painful death or why any sort of tragedy occurs. I only know I have to trust that God's ways are higher than my ways, that He plans good and not evil for my life." She yawned. "Sorry."

"You'd better get to bed. Do you have to work tomorrow morning?" He glanced at the clock. She would only get a few hours sleep if she had to be up for the morning shift.

She nodded. "I'm off to bed. Thanks for waiting up for me."

He blinked. Had he waited up for her? He only wanted to make sure she got home safely . . .

It didn't make any sense. But he couldn't deny the truth of it.

He turned out the lights, checked the door and strode into his room. Jessie slept peacefully, his arm now completely healed. Without any help from a nurse or doctor. Sure, Boothe was happy that medical people had helped save that injured family. And if Emma played a part in it, well, he was sure it made her feel good.

If only he could believe in God's goodness and help as plainly as she. But he couldn't. God didn't take care of everyone. And everything did not work out for good. Which left a man no choice but to handle things on his own.

Despite the late hour, it took him a long

time to fall asleep. He woke with a start thinking it was the middle of the night, but a glance at the clock revealed morning had arrived.

He hurried into his clothes and dashed downstairs to stoke up the fire. In the kitchen he put on the coffee, pulled a frying pan from the cupboard and sliced strips of bacon.

"Morning."

At Emma's cheerful voice, he jerked around. Half-moon shadows darkened the skin under her eyes, but she grinned and seemed full of energy.

"Shouldn't you be tired?" He'd had to force himself from his own warm bed.

She stretched her arms over her head. "Nothing like a good night's sleep to refresh. Coffee ready yet? Maybe you should have some."

He filled her cup and poured himself some of the brew. Emma's eyes fairly burst with teasing as she watched him over the brim of her cup.

One sip and he began to feel better. At least he preferred to think it was the coffee and not her smile. Deciding it was too early for deciphering his feelings, he hummed as he turned back to the bacon.

Sunday dawned cold and crisp. A light dusting of snow teased of a break in the drought. Boothe prepared for church. He wanted Jessie to know about God. He wanted God to protect Jessie. And so he went to the service even though he no longer believed as easily and unquestioningly as he once had.

Pastor Douglas's speech was halting. He sometimes fumbled for words, and Boothe remembered Emma said the man had a stroke. It hadn't taken Boothe long to discover the man had a favorite theme — God's faithfulness — and Boothe learned early to take his thoughts elsewhere during the sermon.

This Sunday was no different.

"My text," Pastor Douglas began, "is from Philippians chapter four verse four. 'Rejoice in the Lord always: and again I say, Rejoice.' How many of us have asked 'how'? How, Lord, are we to rejoice when things are going terribly wrong?"

Boothe shifted his mind to other things in order to block out the words. Yet the one word, *how?*, kept calling to him. He didn't, he tried to convince himself, need an answer. He had his own. *It wasn't possible.*

The pastor paused for prayer. "Let us lay our concerns before the Lord so He can speak to us in our need." Among the things he laid before the Lord was the family hurt in the accident. It seemed many of the congregation knew them and a couple of sobs rent the quietness as Pastor Douglas prayed. For a moment after his "amen," the man didn't speak.

"How can we rejoice when a senseless accident leaves a family struggling to survive, when children lay injured and hurting? For each of us, the answer might come in different ways at different times."

Boothe strained forward in his seat, barely breathing as he waited for Pastor Douglas to provide an answer — one enabling Boothe to recapture the assurance of faith he'd once known.

"It's possible only if we forget the past and look ahead to the right things."

Boothe closed his mind. Forget Alyse, forget the pain she suffered? He couldn't even if he wanted to. And he didn't. He didn't ever want to forget what happened when a man turned over the care of his loved ones to someone else.

Boothe shifted so his gaze wasn't drawn to the front of the church. Emma sat ahead of him, across the aisle, and he studied her. She stared straight ahead, nodding slightly at something the pastor said. For a change, she'd pinned her thick hair around her head. Her brown hat sat in the middle of the bouffant roll, a fuzzy feather of some sort waving as she moved her head.

He'd seen little of her the past few days. She'd worked late four days in a row. Last night she came home early, but when she sat down to help with the gifts, Boothe excused himself and went to the basement to cut out some toys. The day of the accident, or more correctly, the morning after, he'd realized how far he'd allowed his thoughts to wander. Emma was a nurse, which was reason enough to avoid feeling anything for her, but she was controlling as well. She organized the residents at the house as completely as she organized the toy-making project. He knew he wasn't being entirely fair in his judgment. It seemed they gladly let her organize them. But being annoyed about it proved the only way to keep himself from admitting the thoughts buried deep under his resentment and anger. The truth was he craved her company. And admitting it caused his stomach to clench.

■ ■ ■ ■

Emma paused inside the door to the boardinghouse and listened — something she never used to do. And totally unnecessary. Boothe wouldn't be home from work for an hour or more. But there she stood, even forgetting to close the door, which she did now with a quiet click. It was silly, she scolded herself, to be prepared to slip up to her room if she heard his voice. She paid to live here. She could come and go in any of the public rooms as she wished.

But she didn't want to encounter Boothe. For days he'd been terse around her to the point her skin prickled if they were in the same room. For the life of her, she couldn't explain why he had gone from laughing and waiting up for her to treating her like she had the plague.

Her memories dipped back to that night. That special night when he'd waited up for her. At least it had felt special to her. And they'd talked about what they each believed. She'd allowed herself to think something had changed between them. Despite her weariness, her heart had reacted in a foolish, eager way when he poured her tea and made sure she had something to eat.

The next day he seemed glad to see her. Their eyes connected for a beat longer than usual.

But now this . . . this cold distance. She couldn't find a reason for it. Except he'd reverted to his earlier opinion and what he thought of her being a nurse. Though she thought saving all those involved in the accident should cause him to change his mind about the medical community. The father and two older children had gone home. The mother remained with her younger daughter.

Emma wondered why Boothe didn't acknowledge the benefit of medical help in this case. The whole family might have perished or if a couple of them had survived, it would have been with major handicaps. Dr. Phelps had done an excellent job, and the nursing skills of herself and others on staff played a huge role. But she might as well save her breath as say all this to Boothe. He wanted to believe what he wanted to believe. Perhaps it was easier than dealing with reality. She'd faced that choice, too, but accepting the facts of life, adjusting to them, doing what one could to deal with them made a lot more sense in her mind then clinging to futile denial and unfair blame.

And that's what she needed to do now — accept the reality of the situation and be practical about it.

She heard Ada and Jessie's voices in the kitchen. None other. So she stepped into the room.

"Hi, Jessie." She ruffled his hair. Thankfully the boy didn't share his father's opinion of her. They had become good friends. "Ada, how are you? Can I help with anything?"

"No, my dear. Sit down and relax. I just made tea."

Emma poured a cupful, then at Jessie's begging, prepared him one of mostly milk. "How was school today?"

He shrugged.

Emma chuckled. She guessed Jessie would never admit to liking school. "Did you do anything fun?"

"We're building a snow fort."

The needed snow had finally come, reluctantly, miserly, but the wind created drifts the children enjoyed.

"Do you know your part for the Christmas concert?"

"I'm a star that burns warm," he repeated in a singsongy voice. "Ruthie gets to say she's a star that shines bright." Jessie crossed his arms over his chest and glowered. "I don't want to burn. I want to shine."

Emma blinked and shot a surprised glance at Ada, who sputtered her tea. Laughing, Emma pulled Jessie into her arms and hugged him. "Oh, honey, burning is good. Think of how nice the flames are in a fire. Warm and dancing." She grinned at Ada, her eyes burning with delight at Jessie's reasoning. Or — her grin widened as she thought of Jessie's Christmas recitation — were her eyes shining? "You're so sweet," she murmured against the boy's hair.

He leaned into her shoulder. His arms stole around her neck.

She closed her eyes and breathed in his little boy scent of wool, milk and the soul-deep need for hugging. Boothe hugged him lots but Jessie missed his mother's hugs or maybe his aunt's. She'd never heard him ask for his mother but often for Auntie Vera.

Suddenly aware of how she clung to the child, she drew a shaky breath and eased out of his clasp.

"Will you read to me?" he asked, his eyes large with earnestness.

How could she refuse either of them the pleasure? "Did you have a book in mind?"

He nodded and hurried to the cupboard. He brought back the Joseph storybook and laid it on her lap, leaning heavily against her shoulder as she read.

Soon she finished and closed the book. Glancing at the clock she realized Boothe would soon be home. She handed Jessie the book. "Put it away when you're done."

"I will." He turned pages, studying the pictures.

"I have to change." She hurried to her room where she remained long after she'd removed her uniform and put on a sweater and warm skirt, struggling with her emotions. She fluctuated between disappointment at the way Boothe had pulled back, reverting to his cold demeanor, and anger at herself for caring. Like a sprinkling of snow over it all lay her deep-seated longing to love Jessie. But she couldn't let herself. Not like she wanted. *Lord, I want to be obedient to You. I want to accept my responsibilities wholeheartedly, with nothing causing me to wish for anything else. But Jessie is such a sweet boy.*

The feel of his arms about her neck, the way his hair tickled her cheek —

She allowed one fleeting, honest emotion to surface.

She wanted to be more to Jessie than a fellow boarder.

More to Boothe than —

She gasped.

Oh, God. Forgive me for wanting things I can't have. In You I trust. I know somehow You will take the mess of my life and turn it for good. Be with Mom and Dad and Sid. Keep them safe.

The outer door clicked. A few minutes later, it clicked again. She heard the murmur of voices, footsteps going up and down the stairs, hall doors opening and closing. Four times the outer door clicked. Everyone must be home now. Certain she heard Boothe's voice, she stayed in her room, her Bible open, her finger at a verse. *No man having put his hand to the plow, and looking back, is fit for the kingdom of God.*

She hadn't asked for things to be the way they were. If she could undo one hour —

But she couldn't. She'd accepted her responsibility in what happened, had put her hand to the plow and would not turn back. But there came times like now when regrets assaulted her.

Only one thing gave her the strength to put aside her regrets — she believed God had His plans for good even in the midst of trials.

Thank You, Father. In You I trust.

Someone rang the little bell signaling supper. Smiling, her heart calmed with God's peace, she closed her Bible and went downstairs.

Jessie rushed to her side. "Where you been?"

"Upstairs."

"I want you to look at my elbow. It hurts." He pulled up his sleeve and crooked his arm toward her.

She saw no sign of injury and leaned over to run her fingers along the bone. "Where does it hurt?"

"There."

She moved her fingers to a different spot. "How about here?"

"Yes."

Wherever she pressed his arm, he said it hurt. "I think I know exactly what it needs." She touched her lips to his elbow and made a loud kissing noise. "Best medicine in the world. Is it better now?"

Jessie nodded. "I think so." He rolled down his sleeve and faced her. "Thank you for fixing it."

Boothe stepped into the hall. His eyes narrowed. "Jessie, are you bothering Miss Emma?" From the thunderous look on Boothe's face, she wondered if he'd heard the word *medicine.*

She glanced at Jessie's crestfallen face and wanted to hug him. "He wasn't bothering me. Not at all." She wanted to grab Boothe and shake him hard. She had no intention of interfering with the medical care of his son. The kind of medicine she'd just dispensed didn't require any training, only a little sympathy and understanding. "Didn't I hear the supper bell?" She swept past Boothe without giving him another look. Let him think what he wanted. Unless he forbid it, she would continue to give out free hugs and kisses to Jessie.

Jessie needed her as much as she needed him.

She tried not to feel the strain of Boothe's silent disapproval over supper and refused to blame herself. She didn't need his dark, glowering looks to warn her she flirted with impossibilities when she thought of him as more than Ada's nephew and helper.

Jessie hopped around from foot to foot as the boarders cleaned the kitchen. "I can help."

"You sure can," Betty said. "You can put this pot in the cupboard for me."

Jessie rushed to do it. "What else?"

Emma wondered why this sudden urgency. She glanced at Boothe to see if he understood, but he met her gaze and gave a tiny shrug.

"Are you all done?" Jessie demanded a few minutes later as Boothe wiped the counter and Emma hung the tea towels on a line behind the stove.

"I think we are." Boothe said. "What's your hurry? Do you have homework?"

But Jessie rushed from the room before Boothe finished.

"He has something up his sleeve." Emma laughed nervously hoping her words wouldn't remind Boothe of the little scene in the hall. She wasn't sure how much he'd seen or heard.

Before Boothe could respond, a beaming Jessie returned bearing the box of dominoes. "Let's play."

Emma smiled at the eager boy. "You and your daddy have lots of fun."

Before she could slip out of the room, Jessie grabbed her hand. "I want all of us to play — you and me and Daddy."

At the pleading in his eyes, the quiver of his mouth, she stopped and faced Boothe, silently seeking his decision.

He studied his son then slowly brought his gaze to her, uncertain, as if he wanted to refuse but couldn't bear to disappoint Jessie — the same confusion she struggled with. She wanted to spend time with Jessie but Boothe had not shown any desire for her company in a long time. She couldn't quite pinpoint when it had happened or why. She wished she knew the why. But whether she did or not, she wouldn't refuse Jessie unless Boothe made it clear he didn't want her there.

Finally, Boothe's eyes softened and he smiled. "I could use some fun. How about you?"

She grinned, fearing her sudden rush of joy would make her glow. Why did she feel as if her heart had suddenly been freed from a short tether? "I think I could stand some fun, too."

They played a game of matching like-ends on the tiles then Jessie insisted on a game of "knock 'em down." He laughed so hard each time the row of tiles fell that Emma laughed, too. Her enjoyment doubled when Boothe's laughter joined in. Suddenly she couldn't look at Boothe without her eyes feeling hot.

Later, as Boothe tucked Jessie into bed, she put out brown wrapping paper. The gifts were finished. They only had to be wrapped for the upcoming party.

Betty poked her head in the room. "Is Jessie gone?"

"He's off to bed."

Betty ducked back to the front room.

"Come on, people. We have work to do."

The others came in.

"Let's set up a system," Emma said. "We can work around the table in teams. One wrap, the other mark the gift for a boy or girl." She laid out scissors and string. Ed made sure he paired up with Betty. Don and Sarah went to the other side of the table. Loretta and Ada carried in the forty pairs of mittens.

"These are lovely," Emma said. The others added comments of praise.

"We'll just be in the way," Ada said. "Come on, Loretta."

"How can I help?"

She jumped at Boothe's question. She didn't expect him to join them. Lately, he'd found reasons to avoid the gathering, though he continued to make toys on his own. "You could —" She glanced around the table.

"He'll have to be your partner," Sarah said, barely taking her attention from the doll she wrapped.

Emma's heart turned into a heavy lump. She didn't want to work with him. She'd been far too aware of him as they played with Jessie. She'd hoped for a respite from her stubborn longings. Having put her hand to the plow, she would not look back. Nor wish for things not available to her. Not that Boothe represented those things. Her mouth grew dry as she tried to speak.

Thankfully, Betty rescued her. "You can work at the end of the table."

"Sure." She grabbed a roll of brown paper and a ball of string. "Do you want to wrap or write on the parcel?" She avoided looking at him as she edged closer, realizing with a burst of alarm how narrow the end of the table was they'd have to share.

"I'll let you wrap." He stood beside her, so close she smelled coal dust from his last trip down to the basement. He must have put an awful lot of coal on the fire because her skin felt overly warm.

"Fine." She grabbed a pair of mittens and struggled to fold the paper around them neatly.

Betty noticed and laughed. "Sure hope you're better at bandaging then you are at wrapping."

Emma laughed, too, her voice high and nervous. She made herself stop, sucked in air and held it, trying to calm her jittery heartbeat.

"I got started wrong." She smoothed the paper and started over. She grabbed a length of string to tie the bundle shut. The string knotted. She struggled to undo the tangle.

"Let me help." Boothe's low voice seemed full of amusement, which only increased her discomfort. Their fingers brushed as he pulled the string from her and sorted it out. A flame of embarrassment shot straight up her arm and burned into her heart like a raging fire. Why was she letting his nearness, his touch make her act so foolishly?

Because, she admitted, she had opened the door to her dreams and desires the first time she saw him on the street and noted his tenderness with Jessie. It reminded her of everything she wanted and couldn't have.

She accepted that some things could never be hers. Her commitment would be required the rest of her life. She wrenched shut a mental door, grabbed the scissors and cut the thread as Boothe successfully tied the parcel.

If he wondered why her hands jerked as she worked, he gave no indication. In fact, he seemed perfectly at ease as if he felt none of the chafing tension between them. Yet he could hardly miss it. Sparks fairly danced in the air at the end of the table they shared.

She sighed in relief when all the gifts were wrapped and stacked in boxes ready to be

delivered to the church. "Thank you, everyone."

Sarah, in her soft gentle way, spoke. "It's
as much our responsibility as yours or the
Douglases to see the children of the community get gifts at Christmas."

"That's a fact," Boothe said.

Emma shot him a look. Darted it away so
fast her head spun but not before she saw a
gleam in his eyes she couldn't interpret.

Ed, Don and Boothe stored the boxes in
the hall closet, out of sight until they could
be delivered.

Emma clasped her hands together. The
job had united them each evening. Now she
felt at loose ends. She should be glad.
Boothe would no longer feel he had to
spend his time with her — them, she corrected herself.

She would no longer have any reason to
expect to see him for more than mealtime.

But she wasn't a bit glad. Something good
and precious had ended. And she didn't
want it to. "What about tea and cookies?"

"Good idea," Ed said as he withdrew from
the depths of the closet. His gaze lingered
on Betty, and Emma felt a burst of sympathy
for the man. It hurt to care about someone
when it was futile or foolish.

Emma tightened her jaw. She had no

room for foolishness. Time to get on with the realities of her life. With determined steps, she filled the kettle and put it to boil.

Chapter Seven

Boothe hummed as he headed back to the boardinghouse. He pulled his collar up and closed the neck of his coat more tightly against the nasty bite of the cold. He wouldn't mind the bitter temperature so much if it brought more snow.

Life had settled into a familiar routine of work, time spent with Jessie and helping Aunt Ada care for the house. Since the gifts were completed, the boarders returned to sitting in the front room as Emma read aloud. He hated to admit it, but he enjoyed the evenings. Emma had a good reading voice. The story she read held compelling qualities even if the simplistic, unflinching faith of the characters bothered him. If only life could be as uncomplicated as it had been when he kissed Alyse goodbye in the morning, went to work, kissed her again upon his return and tossed Jessie in the air until he squealed. Do the same thing six days a week and go to church on Sunday with a wife at his side, a son in his arms and his faith intact.

After a period of whining about school and complaining about missing Aunt Vera, Jessie now seemed happy enough. His change was due, in part, to Emma's influence. Boothe had mixed feelings about her involvement with his son, but he didn't want to spoil the gentle contentment of today by analyzing the situation.

He stepped inside the boardinghouse and shrugged out of his winter coat. A few letters lay on the small hall table, and he rifled through them to see if any were for him. His name stood out, stark and black, on a long linen-weave envelope. The return address gave the name of a legal firm back in Lincoln. The skin across the back of his neck tingled as he pulled his pocketknife out, slit open the envelope and drew out the single sheet of heavy paper.

He read the contents twice. Skipping all the fancy words, it plain and simply said Vera and Luke had filed for custody of Jessie.

His arms grew numb. The inside of his head felt scraped hollow. His heart pressed against the soles of his shoes. They wanted to adopt Jessie. He jammed the letter back into the envelope, not caring that he crumpled them both in the process, and stared at the closed door. He thought this was over. He thought he'd put an end to it by moving to Favor.

But he was wrong.

"Daddy, you're home." Jessie raced to him, pulling on his arm and demanding attention.

Boothe shook free. "I have to go out again. See if you can help Aunt Ada." He grabbed his coat and hat and stepped into the cold. He strode to the street before he realized he carried his coat and jerked it on. He jammed the hat to his head and half ran, half staggered toward the center of town.

He reached the office he subconsciously sought just as a man pulled the door shut and turned the key in the lock.

Boothe rushed to his side. "Are you the lawyer?"

"I am." The man looked wary, and Boothe guessed the man must think him mad.

"I have to talk to you immediately."

"My office hours are over. Come back tomorrow." The man started to walk away.

"Wait, mister. This is too important. They want to take my son."

The lawyer paused, and Boothe dug the tattered letter from his pocket. "Here, read

132

it. Tell me what to do."

The lawyer hesitated then nodded. "Come inside."

Boothe jerked off his hat and twisted it. "Thank you." He practically trod on the man's heels as he followed him into the small office.

"Sit." The lawyer slipped out of his topcoat and waved toward a straight-backed chair. He went around the desk and sat in a creaky, wooden armed chair. "Let's start with the basics. I'm lawyer Ashby Milton and you are . . . ?"

"Boothe Wallace. It's about my son."

"Pleased to make your acquaintance." Ashby held out a hand.

Boothe shoved the letter into it, then realized the man meant to shake hands. "Sorry." He stuck out his hand and they shook.

Ashby settled back, pulled a leather eyeglass case from his inside pocket, adjusted his lapels, hooked the spectacles over one ear and then the other, sliding them up and down his nose until he seemed happy with the position. Only then did he carefully pull the letter from the envelope and unfold it.

Boothe barely contained his impatience at the needless delay. "They can't do it, can they?" Afraid they could, he added, "How

133

can I stop them?"

Ashby harrumphed and smoothed the letter to the top of his desk. "They allege they have a good home, are well off and able to provide extras for the child whereas you —" He checked the letter. "Have no home, no job and no wife. Is that correct?"

"It was, but I work at White's garage now and we live with my aunt. She owns Ada's Boardinghouse."

"Fine woman." He harrumphed again. "No wife?"

"I'm a widower."

"So who cares for the child when you're at work?"

"Jessie. His name is Jessie. I take him to school, and Aunt Ada is there when he gets home."

"Isn't your aunt rather, well, old?"

Boothe sat forward. This conversation was not going how he wanted. "She's not too old to run a busy boardinghouse. I guess she's not too old to watch a six-year-old child for an hour or two. Besides, Emma Spencer is often around to spend time with him." He never thought he'd be grateful for her interference.

"Mr. Wallace, let me be quite honest with you. Judges favor a two-parent family, especially if they have a permanent home and are well off. It seems in the best interest of the child, wouldn't you agree?"

Boothe jerked forward and planted his fists on the desktop, not caring that he almost tipped over a fine gold-encased clock. The lawyer reached out and straightened it. "No, I don't agree. He's *my* son. He belongs with me."

"I understand your emotions but let's be practical. Your job could be gone tomorrow. Your aunt Ada isn't a young woman. You see how the judge will view this?"

Boothe sank back. Desperation sucked life from his heart. "So what do you suggest I do?"

"It depends on what you're willing to do to keep your son."

"I'm willing to do anything."

"Then I suggest you find a wife. A judge wouldn't be likely to take your son if you were married."

"A wife? I don't know anyone I want to marry." But his mind flooded with pictures of a practical nurse with heavy blond hair in a thick bun and brown eyes that shifted through a range of emotions. Emma? She practically bolted from a room when he entered.

"It's my best advice. I'd give it serious consideration if you want to keep your son."

Ashby removed his spectacles and slid them into the leather case. He again pulled the lapels of his suit into precise alignment then stood. "I can do no more. It's up to you to help yourself."

Knowing he'd been dismissed, Boothe lurched to his feet. "A wife?" An absurd idea.

He realized Ashby waited at the door. He thanked the lawyer, planted his hat on his head and stepped into the cold. Slowly his thoughts cleared.

He'd do whatever he must to keep Jessie. Even marry. He considered the idea, turning it over and over, pushing it into various shapes to see how it felt. A marriage of convenience held certain appeal. A home again. A family again. All without emotional pain. But who would agree to such a thing? He ignored the face laughing at him in his thoughts. Emma would be his last choice.

There was Betty, of course, but she was young and full of dreams of travel and adventure. Sarah, she was older — perhaps too old — and so quiet she scared him. Whenever he talked to her, he got the feeling she'd burst into tears if he raised his voice a fraction. She wasn't what he needed. He needed someone —

Practical.

The word slapped against his brain. Emma and practical were synonymous.

His steps lagged as he let himself explore that direction. Emma would see the advantages of a marriage of convenience. Although she didn't seem to hold Boothe in high regard — more like an unwelcome infection — she showed genuine affection for Jessie.

The wind caught at his collar and shivered down his neck. He picked up his pace. He'd ask her. For Jessie's sake. She would see the practicality of such an arrangement.

Now to plan a time to broach the subject. But when he reached the boardinghouse, he had come up with not one good idea of how to approach her. Not even a half good one. For that matter, he hadn't dredged up even a bad idea. It had been far too long since he'd courted a woman. And with Alyse it hadn't been so much courting on his part as hanging about with her brother, Luke.

Luke was his friend, or so he'd thought. That Luke supported Vera in trying to claim his son seemed the final insult. He'd trusted them to help care for Jessie — not steal him away.

He crunched his teeth together. He would find a way to get Emma alone and propose to her, though he supposed propose was hardly the right word. More like offer a practical proposition.

Emma stood over the stove as he stepped into the house, Jessie hovering at her side. He turned at Boothe's entrance. "Miss Emma's making me hot chocolate."

Boothe assessed Emma as if he'd never seen her before. Her features were dainty, her eyes framed by dark lashes that gave warmth to her face like fur lining in a pair of mittens. The smiles she reserved for Jessie seemed to come from a golden light within. She'd make a good mother for his son.

He almost blurted out his plan right there in the kitchen until he realized Emma had asked him something. "Sorry?"

"I asked if you wanted some hot chocolate, too?"

"Oh, yes. Sounds good." He was as awkward and confused as he'd been at nineteen.

She filled three mugs and set them on the table. She and Jessie grabbed chairs and sat down. He fumbled with the chair closest to him and managed to get himself seated.

"How was your day?"

Jessie answered. "Only two more days until the school concert. Then I don't have to go for two whole weeks." He sighed expansively.

Boothe shifted his gaze to Emma. He'd

really meant the question for her.

Her eyes narrowed before she lowered her gaze.

"And you?" he prodded.

She shot him a look ripe with disbelief. "It was fine."

He understood her hesitation. He'd been pretty forceful about his dislike of the medical profession as a whole. But he was prepared to overlook it in Emma's case. "That's good." He felt her uneasy stillness. No doubt she found his behavior as strange as he found it embarrassing.

He gulped his hot chocolate, gasped as it burned his mouth.

"You have to blow on it. Like this —" Jessie illustrated "— before you drink it."

"*Now* you tell me." Boothe waved his hand at his open mouth to cool his tongue.

Jessie and Emma glanced at each other and attempted to hide their giggles.

Boothe stopped trying to cool his mouth and grasped the hot cup between his palms. Now. Now, he told himself. Do it. He looked squarely at Emma. "What are your plans for the evening?"

She turned from grinning at Jessie. "I told the Douglases I'd decorate the church. Why do you ask?"

He shrugged. "No reason." Did he expect

she would be available because he suddenly had a burning need to talk to her? "Could you use some help?"

Her mouth dropped open. She shut it with an audible click. She mouthed words silently and finally got them out. "Are you offering?"

"I might be of some use."

"It would go faster with help."

Jessie bounced forward. "Can I help, too?"

"It's a school night, son." He hated to disappoint Jessie but this was all about what was best for him. He returned his gaze to Emma. "Can we go after he goes to bed?"

"Certainly." She lifted one hand, and shook her head as if confused.

The church was warm. A naked pine tree stood in one corner. Someone had put boxes on the front pew. Emma hurried to them and started to pull out tinsel, red bells and fragile balls. She lifted a golden garland over her head and laughed. "I love this job."

Boothe hung back. He'd been nervous and jumpy all evening and hoped no one noticed. Even as he tucked Jessie into bed, he'd been trying to think how to ask Emma the question. He could hardly wait to be alone with her. But now he couldn't think why he'd been so anxious for the moment to arrive or how he'd spring the question.

"Here." Emma handed him a box of bells. "Hang those on the tree while I put up the balls."

He knew from doing this with Alyse that he had to balance the placement and, anxious to please Emma, studied the tree before he placed the first bell then he stepped back for more study before he put up the second.

Emma laughed. "Do you want a yardstick to measure it?"

He grimaced. "I'm just trying to do a good job."

"Let's be practical here. We have to get the job done tonight, not next year."

Practical. What he intended to propose was simply that. He tried to hang the bells faster while keeping them balanced. Emma scurried around dotting balls in between the bells all the time talking about how happy the children would be with their presents, how this was her first year celebrating Christmas in Favor. She paused and stared into space. "I hope I can make it home for Christmas Day."

He realized he knew nothing about the woman he planned to ask to marry him. "Do you have a large family?"

"No, only my parents and my brother, Sid."

"They must miss you."

She returned to her task. "No more than I miss them, but I can help them more by working."

"Where do they live?"

"On a farm in North Dakota."

"They've been affected by the drought?"

"It's been awful for them. They haven't grown enough for seed the last three years. They wouldn't have enough money for food and coal without my help." She drew in a long breath. "What about you? Where is your family?"

"My parents are both dead now. My father died when I was nineteen, my mother five years later. No brothers or sisters."

"That must be lonely. No family."

"Alyse — that was my wife's name — had family. Her parents and a brother and sister-in-law live in Lincoln. That's why we were living there."

She straightened from tucking a bell to a lower branch. "Why did you leave?"

"No job. Lost my apartment. Aunt Ada said she could use some help and give us a roof over our head." It seemed like a perfect opening to pop the question. Instead, he said, "And things weren't going good."

"Here, help me wind these garlands around the tree." She held the end of one toward him.

He took it and let her wrap the lower branches while he wrapped the taller ones.

"Now the angel for the top."

He looked at the tree. "Do we have a ladder?"

"I don't know. Would a chair work?" She hurried to the back room and returned with one.

He pulled it as close as possible to the tree and stepped up. She handed him the white robed angel. He could barely reach the top. He stretched an inch more and dropped the angel into place just as the chair scooted away. He leaped aside to keep from falling into the tree and crashed into Emma.

She staggered back, grunting under his assault.

He grasped her shoulders to steady both of them as they struggled to regain their balance. He held her arms and looked into her wide, startled eyes. She really was quite beautiful. She'd make a fine wife. "Will you marry me?"

CHAPTER EIGHT

Emma broke from his grasp and stepped backward until a pew blocked her retreat. "Are you crazy?"

Boothe scrubbed his hand over his chin, the rasping of his whiskers scratching along her nerves. He'd been acting strangely all evening. But this was the crowning act.

She laughed nervously. "I know you don't mean it, but it's not funny to pretend."

"No, I mean it. I just didn't mean for it to come out like that."

"We don't even like each other. Why would you want to marry me?" At the untruthfulness of her words, heat raced up her veins leaving a hot spot on her cheeks. She'd tried to tell herself otherwise, but she liked him. Might even admit she'd grown slightly fond of him. Okay. Truth time. She might even be a little attracted to him. Had been since her first glimpse, even though she knew it to be foolish.

He took a step closer and stopped, correctly reading the alarm in her eyes. "I like you just fine."

"I'm a nurse. Have you forgotten?"

He hesitated. "Well, as nurses go, you seem to be a good one."

She snorted in a most unladylike fashion. "I'm thrilled to hear that."

"Surely we could work around that."

"I think not. Can you imagine how we'd disagree if I thought one of us or —" Her cheeks burned. She'd been about to say one of our children. Marriage and children went hand in hand but she couldn't say it aloud. "If I thought someone needed medical attention?"

"I'm desperate."

"Well, thanks. I guess." Just what she'd always dreamed of — the last pick of the crop to someone who was desperate. She edged along the pew until she came to the end and prepared to bolt.

"Wait. Listen to what I have to say." He pulled a battered envelope from his back pocket.

Nothing he said would change the fact they were as unsuited for each other as cat and mouse, yet she hesitated, wanting — hoping — for something to persuade her otherwise. She sucked in steadying air, sought in vain for reason knowing nothing he said would change the reality of her responsibilities.

He waved her toward a pew and she cautiously took a seat. He plopped down beside her. "This is a letter from a lawyer back in Lincoln informing me that my brother-in-law and his wife intend to adopt Jessie."

She gasped. "How can that be?"

He rattled the paper and looked bleak. "I needed help after Alyse died and Vera offered. Only then she wanted to keep Jessie. I thought she'd forget about it when we moved away." A shudder shivered up his neck.

Emma reached for him, pressed her palm to his shoulder. How did a man face the possibility of losing his son? "Surely they don't have a chance?"

He slowly brought his gaze toward her. At the look of despair in his eyes, her throat pinched closed and she scrubbed her lips together to stop the cry of pain begging to explode from her mouth.

"I went to see the lawyer in town, Ashby Milton, and he says the courts favor people who have money and their own home, but especially both a father and mother. He says my best chance is to get married."

She settled back, affronted to be no more

146

than a means to an end, and yet, would her dreams and hopes never leave her alone? "And I was the only person you could think of?"

He snorted. "Do you see Betty or Sarah filling the role? Besides —" He shrugged. "You're fond of Jessie."

A burning mix of sympathy and annoyance shot through her. She withdrew her hand from his shoulder even though she ached to comfort him. She sat up straight, folded her hands together in her lap and forced reluctant words from her mouth. "Yes, I'm fond of Jessie but I can't marry — not you or anyone."

He narrowed his eyes. "Something wrong with you?"

She spared him a squinty-eyed look. "I have to help my family."

His breath released in a low whistle. "Whew. There for a minute . . . Never mind. I understand whatever you send your family each month is probably keeping them alive and fed right now, but the drought will end. Maybe we'll get lots of snow this winter and enough rain next spring —"

She cut him off. "They'll still need my help." She'd owe them for the rest of her life for what had happened.

"I don't understand. What about the

farm? What about your brother?"

She leaned over as pain shot through her middle. She wanted him to stop asking questions. Each one drove a rusty spike of regret through her mind, reminding her —

"How old is your brother?"

"Sid is a year younger than I am." She thrust out the words before she had time to consider and instantly wished she could pull them back.

"Well. There you go. You're what — twentysomething?"

"Twenty-four," she mumbled. *Stop. Please stop. Don't make me think about it.*

"A good age. I'm twenty-nine myself. So your brother — Sid, right?" He waited for her slight nod. "He's twenty-three. He can help them until the drought ends. Then things will get better."

She burst to her feet and strode away then stopped, drew in a deep breath and slowly turned to face him. "It's not that simple. I'm sorry but I can't marry you."

He sank over his knees as if his spine had melted. "Then I'm going to lose Jessie."

She couldn't let that happen. But how could she prevent it? Not through marriage. She scrambled to think of an available woman. Two unmarried women sprang to mind but she quickly dismissed each. One was surely too mean-natured to be a mother to Jessie. The second — she tried to find some reason for discounting Marissa other than the fact she was far too pretty. Yes, she found it. Marissa was self-absorbed. Not a good match for Boothe and certainly not a good mother for Jessie.

She scrambled for other solutions as Boothe sat with his head in his hands. "What about God?"

"You think He'll help me?" Boothe's voice dripped bitter disbelief. "Does He care if I keep Jessie or not?" He gave a dispirited shrug.

"What I meant is I could never be unequally yoked with someone who doesn't believe."

He sat up and stared at her. "It isn't that I don't believe, only that my trust has been shattered of late. I'm trying to reconcile my belief in God's love and goodness with what's happening in my life."

They stared at each other as Emma considered his words, his offer of marriage, the consequence of refusing him, the impossibility of accepting. And yet . . .

To think of being Boothe's wife.

A chance to be loved and cherished. To have children. To have and to hold a man —

Heat burned up her limbs and pooled in her cheeks. Why was she allowing such errant thoughts? Why was she tormenting herself with impossible dreams? Even if she didn't have her family to consider, Boothe's proposal had nothing to do with love and mutual care. He only wanted a mother for Jessie.

Finally, Boothe looked away. He folded the letter and returned it to the envelope, stood and shoved it in his back pocket. "All I can do is hope and pray the judge will look favorably on me but I fear —" He stopped as his voice grew husky. "I fear I'm going to lose my son." His words came as a tortured whisper. He turned, his mouth drawn into a thin line, his eyes dark with despair. "I'm begging you, Emma, marry me. Help me keep my son."

She shook her head, as filled with misery as he. "I can't." Her eyes stung with tears. "I wish I could."

He nodded slowly. "I guess that's it then . . . unless . . . maybe we don't have to marry."

She gasped at the indecency of his suggestion.

He gave a snort as he realized how she'd interpreted his remarks. "I mean perhaps we can pretend to be engaged until after the court date. If the judge thinks I'm to marry, he might rule in my favor. And then we can go our separate ways."

Emma stared at him. "A *pretend* engagement?" Her initial shock gave way to another thought. It might be possible. A great hollow disappointment sucked at her thought. She wanted more. So much more. Impossibly more.

"Just until the court date."

"Which is when?" She couldn't believe she even considered it.

"Middle of February."

"Almost two months away."

"You think we could pretend to be in love for a few weeks?"

Oh, if only he guessed how easy it would be for her. She closed her eyes and despaired at how fickle her heart proved to be.

"For Jessie," Boothe added.

She opened her eyes. "I can't lie."

"We'll be engaged. You don't have to lie about anything. We won't be the first couple to change our minds before the wedding."

"I don't know what I'd say to my parents. They're counting on me."

"Assure them we won't marry until they no longer need your help."

It was all she could do not to sob. That time would never come, and she had no one to blame but herself.

She considered the idea as something warm and unfamiliar came from somewhere deep inside her. It would only be pretend but to allow herself to dream if even for a few weeks . . . "Very well. A pretend engagement until you go to court."

Before she realized what he meant to do, he swept her into a hug, lifting her off her feet as he swung her about, laughing. He put her down but kept his arms around her. "I could kiss you." He tipped his head, smiling as he studied her, letting his gaze linger on her hair, making her want to brush it into submission. He shifted his gaze down her cheeks and across her eyes with such intensity she bent her head and quickly, lest she miss any of this delightful exploration, again looked into his face. Before she could think what to do, he lowered his head and captured her mouth in a gentle kiss that slid past her defenses, exposing her dreams to the light of loving. She could love this man. She could and she did. Suddenly she wondered how she'd survive a pretend engagement. How she'd go back to being practical, focused Emma. How she'd accept what her life had to be.

Boothe lifted his head and holding Emma in the circle of his arms, laughed low in his throat. "I think I am a very fortunate man."

She slipped from his grasp. "How are we going to tell the others?"

He pulled her to his side and tucked her arm through his. "When they see you with stars in your eyes and me grinning like a gold mine landed in my lap, I don't think they'll have any trouble believing we've discovered we have enough in common to want to marry."

Emma swallowed back disappointment at his words. Even in pretense he couldn't bear to say the word *love?* And what did she expect? Love did not exist between them — only a fabrication. What possessed her to agree to such a thing? But as he helped her put away the boxes, held her coat as she slipped into it then dropped his arm across her shoulder and gave her a quick hug, she knew she would forever cherish the next few weeks and forever hold them close to her heart. She only hoped they would be enough to satisfy her dreams.

She let a curtain of contentment filter her thoughts as they made their way back to the boardinghouse. Boothe couldn't seem to stop laughing and squeezing her close. The gesture was only gratitude and relief that she'd given him a chance to keep Jessie but her brain ignored the facts; her heart pretended far more than their agreement included.

They burst into the house, laughing as they tried to jostle through the door at the same time. He took her coat and draped it over the banister before he hung his own.

"Let's go tell the others," he whispered.

She hung back. What had she done? How could she deal with this without lying?

He grabbed her hand and pulled her into the center of the front room. "Everyone, we have an announcement."

Six pairs of eyes focused on them and Emma squirmed. She hated deceiving her friends.

He held up their joined hands and laughed. "Emma and I are engaged." He shot her a look of reassurance as if to say he didn't have to lie.

Aunt Ada stared at them. "Well, I'll be."

Loretta nodded. "Good news."

Betty squealed. "I'm not surprised. I've seen the way you look at each other when you think no one is watching."

Emma ducked her head. She thought she'd hidden her interest in Boothe better.

The others offered their congratulations.

"When's the big day?" Betty demanded.

Boothe grinned. "We haven't had time to discuss details."

"I can make the dress," Sarah said.

"We can have the reception here." Ada glanced about the room as if already moving furniture and decorating. "Or if you wait until summer, out in the yard."

Emma lifted her palms to stop all the offers. "Thank you all, but we haven't made any plans yet. We haven't even told our families." She sent Boothe a panic-laced look. There were so many things to figure out. She grabbed his hand and pulled him into the kitchen.

"They'll think we've come to steal some kisses." He studied her mouth as if considering the idea.

She pressed a hand to his chest to hold him at bay. "What are we going to tell my family? What —" she leaned closer and demanded in a harsh whisper "— are we going to tell Jessie?"

He settled back on his heels. "He's going to expect us to get married."

"I don't want to hurt him, but I don't see how we can avoid it."

Boothe's expression hardened. "I can tell him the truth once he's safe with me. He'll understand."

"I hope so. What are you going to tell him in the meantime?"

"The same as I told the others. That we're

155

engaged."

"What am I supposed to say when he asks me questions?"

"Surely you can tell him you care about him and want to help keep him safe. That's the truth, isn't it?"

Emma nodded, all the magic gone as she considered how this would affect Jessie. But she'd done this solely for his sake. To keep him safe, as Boothe said. She sent up a quick prayer for wisdom in handling the situation.

"What are you two doing?" Betty called. "We want to hear more about how this happened."

Emma shot Boothe an annoyed look. "I can hardly wait to see how you handle this." She marched back into the other room, Boothe at her heels.

"Well?" Betty said.

Boothe smiled with all the assurance of a cat licking down the last of the cream. "You could say I fell for her. I was putting the angel on top of the tree when the chair slid and dumped me at her feet. I looked into those beautiful dark eyes and well . . . I did more than fall off the chair." He grinned at Emma.

She couldn't fault him. Not once had he said anything that wasn't true except the part about her beautiful eyes. She only wished he meant it.

"I'm asking you all to keep it a secret until we've had a chance to tell Jessie. We want to do it together." He smiled at Emma with unfamiliar warmth. "But we'll have to wait until we're all home tomorrow afternoon."

He didn't have to wait for her, but the fact he'd thought to do so sneaked past her good intentions and landed in her heart like a dollop of honey.

She whispered a prayer of thanks as she hurried home the next day, certain only God's kindness and intervention kept her from making a mistake at work. Several times she emptied a bedpan or adjusted a bed with her mind elsewhere.

After a guilt-riddled sleep that left her restless and jumpy, she'd faced Boothe at the breakfast table, amid the watchful, curious glances of the others. He'd seemed quite relaxed and even made a point of slipping out to the hall to whisper goodbye as she headed out for work.

For a minute, as he stood close telling her they'd break the news to Jessie as soon as he got home from the garage, she feared he'd kiss her.

Feared he wouldn't.

When he stood back, holding the door as she stepped into the cold, she forcefully reminded herself this was all pretend.

Hours later, returning over the same path, she told herself the same thing. *It's just pretend.*

She stepped into the house. Jessie's voice and Ada's came from the kitchen. She tipped her head and listened. No other voice spoke. Her lungs released. An hour more or less before she'd have to deal with her errant emotions about this pretend engagement.

And before they had to face Jessie.

Time to prepare herself. She called hello into the kitchen then retreated to her bedroom intending to fortify herself with prayer before Boothe came home.

Her Bible lay on the table by her bed, and she sank to the mattress and let the pages fall open where they would. Her eyes fixed on a verse she'd marked for some reason, which now escaped her memory. *Pure religion and undefiled before God and the Father is this, to visit the fatherless and widows in their affliction, and to keep himself unspotted from the world.*

She groaned. Agreeing to this helped out a widower and a child who would otherwise lose his father. She assumed God would be pleased with her doing that. But "unspotted from the world"? Surely it was worldly desires making her ache for even a teasing taste of what she wanted — a husband and a child.

"Lord, God," she whispered, "I want to do this for the right reasons — to help Boothe keep Jessie. Forgive me for all the times my own desires get in the way. Help me keep my good reason firmly in the front of my mind."

When she heard Boothe downstairs, she closed her Bible and put it back in its spot. Her fingers lingered on the cover, and then she went to join Boothe.

He smiled as she entered the kitchen, and despite her promise and prayer from a few minutes ago, her heart lifted in joy at the way his eyes warmed. She drew in a deep breath and denied such feelings. Her lips felt wooden as she returned his smile.

Boothe turned to Jessie. "Come with us, son. We have something to tell you." They walked into the front room. He closed the door to ensure their privacy.

Jessie backed away, his eyes wide with wariness. "What's wrong?"

Boothe waved Emma to the sofa. As soon as she was seated, he sank down beside her and beckoned Jessie.

"You're going to send me away, aren't you?"

Boothe chuckled. "You couldn't be more wrong, son." He took Emma's hand and favored her with another grateful smile. "Miss Emma and I are engaged."

Jessie looked puzzled.

"That's what people do before they get married."

Jessie looked from Boothe to Emma. "You're going to marry my daddy?"

Emma considered her words carefully. She wouldn't lie. "We're engaged." Guilt made her squirm. She hadn't lied with her mouth, but they lived a lie with this pretense.

Jessie stepped closer and studied their faces in turn then gave Boothe an intense look. "Does that mean you love Miss Emma?"

Emma's heart set up an incessant ticking. How would Boothe handle this? She forced herself to look at him, met his suddenly sober gaze.

"That's —"

Jessie threw himself against Emma, wrapping his arms around her neck, burying his face against her shoulder and pinning her arms to her side. "I love you, too, Miss Emma. I prayed you would be my new mommy."

Emma couldn't speak. She loved this boy. She loved his father. And she sensed two out of the three in this room were going to end up paying a high emotional price for this little deception.

Her eyes stung. Her heart turned into a heavy lump of lifeless clay. A sob tore at her throat. She managed to choke it back.

Boothe rubbed Jessie's back. She forced herself to meet his gaze, saw a reflection of her aching regret. Seeing his misery only increased the choking sensation in her throat and she coughed.

Jessie released her from his neck hold, planted himself firmly between them and reached up to wrap his arms around their necks. "This is the best day of my life. The last day of school before Christmas vacation. The concert tonight. And now this. Yup. This is the best day ever."

Emma sniffed and swallowed hard. When he learned the truth, it would no doubt be the worst day of his life.

Jessie bounced to his feet, slammed open the door and raced back to the kitchen where he yelled, "Aunt Ada, did you know my daddy's going to marry Miss Emma?"

Emma twisted her hands in her lap. "I can't do this," she whispered.

Boothe squeezed her hands. "It's harder

than I expected, but I don't know how else to make sure I keep Jessie. And we've gone this far — we can hardly undo things now."

She understood the truth of his words. Having given Jessie a promise, even if only by failing to be truthful, they might as well stick to their plan. He wouldn't be hurt any worse seven or eight weeks from now than he would if they told him the truth now and certainly far less than being taken from his father. "Seems we're stuck in our lie."

"We haven't lied."

"Not by word but we have by our deeds. Is there any difference?"

"I suppose not. I just don't see what else to do."

"I agreed to help you and I'll do so." She pushed to her feet and forced her rubbery limbs to hold her upright as she made her way to the door.

Boothe caught her before she made it out of the room. "No one is going to believe you if you run around with a long face."

She tried a smile, found it shaky.

He turned her to face him. "A newly engaged woman should have stars in her eyes." Before she could think what he meant, he planted a firm kiss on her mouth. He let his lips linger until she forgot the problems of being engaged to this man.

He broke away and studied her. "That's better."

Her cheeks flooded with fire. "Oh —"

He grabbed her hand and pulled her into the hall. "Doesn't feel so bad now, does it?" He led her into the kitchen without giving her a chance to answer.

She suffered through supper and the cleanup afterward without drawing any curious questions, even though she felt edgy and knew she jumped when someone spoke to her. Then she and Boothe accompanied Jessie to the school.

This school was not like the one-room, wooden-frame structure she and Sid had attended. This was an impressive two-story brick building, with a set of wide stairs going up and down from the entryway. There were two classrooms on the lower floor, another on the second plus an auditorium.

Jessie dragged them to a row of chairs. "You sit here. I'll be up there with my teacher." He pointed to the row of squirming little boys and dressed up little girls. "Do I look okay?"

Boothe squeezed his shoulder. "You look fine."

Jessie waited for Emma to say something. She bent over and whispered, "You are the best looking boy in the room."

His chest lifted several inches before he rushed off to join his class.

"What did you tell him?"

Emma told him, pleased when Boothe chuckled.

"You made his day."

"Well, he is. And he looks real fine in that little sweater and dark pants."

Boothe's expression darkened. "Vera insisted on buying the very best."

"Aah." That explained the fancy clothes Jessie wore.

"I won't be able to afford to dress him that well when he outgrows his current set of clothes." Boothe looked troubled as he watched his son.

She squeezed his arm. "I think what you have to give him is far more valuable than pretty clothes."

Slowly he turned toward her. "What do I have to offer him?"

"Your love. And your commitment."

His face relaxed. "Thank you for saying that. It's what counts, isn't it?"

She nodded, and then silence fell on the crowd as a teacher stood on the platform to welcome them.

Jessie's group was among the first to perform.

Emma's heart warmed as she watched the

students line up. Jessie lifted his hand to his shoulder and waved. His teacher signaled him to stop. He lowered his hand but leaned forward to speak to the teacher and in a stage whisper that could be heard in every corner of the room, said, "That's Miss Emma with my daddy. She's going to be my new mommy." He smiled like a bright Christmas star and waved at them.

A sound of amusement rippled across the audience, and dozens of eyes turned to stare at her.

Emma's face felt as if it were about to ignite. She wound her fingers together to keep from covering her cheeks.

Boothe squeezed her hands. His steadying touch sent calming strength to her shuddering mind.

CHAPTER NINE

Boothe felt her quaking. He squeezed her scrunched fists. She put on a good front, but this whole engagement thing put her in an awkward position. He wished there was another way, but he could think of none. He had to keep Vera and Luke from taking Jessie.

He owed Emma immensely for her co-operation with this idea. Right after the court date, he would thank her profusely and end this farce. He squeezed her hands tighter, telling himself they could both walk away unscathed by this whole business. He ignored the little twist in his heart. This slight shift in his feelings toward her was his own fault. Plain and simple, you couldn't kiss a woman without having some sort of reaction. And if his reaction surprised him — well, he would be careful not to kiss her again.

She strained forward, and he realized

Jessie was about to speak his piece.

Jessie beamed enough to rival all the stars in heaven as he said his few words and smiled at them for approval. Boothe nodded, so proud of this scrap of humanity he'd produced he couldn't contain it. He grinned at Emma, saw an answering gleam in her eyes. She truly cared about his son. He turned away as a twinge intruded into his conscience. She wouldn't want to give up Jessie any more than Jessie would want to give her up.

His smile slipped sideways at the thought, but it was only for a short time. They'd all recover.

The other children did their parts, and then each received an orange and a small bundle of candy tied up in brown store paper.

Jessie raced to join them and held out his gifts. "An orange. Auntie Vera used to give me one."

Boothe's mouth watered at the forgotten pleasure. His heart twisted to think he could not provide such luxuries for his son. But he didn't have time to dwell on it, nor enjoy watching Jessie's pleasure at Emma's praise of his performance for well-wishers immediately swarmed them, pumping his hand and surrounding Emma. Some hugged her, others patted her like they all wanted to touch her. He reached for her hand, pulled her to his side, his arm around her shoulders to hold the eager fans at bay. He began to edge toward the door and escape.

A man blocked their path. He pushed his hat to his chest and darted a glance toward Emma. "Nurse Spencer." His voice was barely audible but the word *nurse* shouted through Boothe's mind. It shivered over his memories and scraped across his resentment. He'd vowed to avoid all contact with anyone in the medical profession. He promised himself they could practice on someone else's family. He could never bring himself to forgive the whole works of them for killing Alyse.

Yet he couldn't equate his feelings about medical people with his feelings for Emma. *Which were?* he silently mocked. Gratitude, of course, for her help without which he'd surely lose his son.

The man's words brought Boothe's attention back to the scene before him. "My wife wanted me to say thank you for looking after her when she was so sick."

Emma touched the man's elbow and Boothe gritted his teeth to keep from pulling her arm back.

"How is she, Mr. Anders?"

"Almost good as new." He gave a quick smile. "You saved her life." In a flash of gratitude, the man grabbed Emma's hand. "You are a fine nurse."

Boothe stiffened and fought the desire to plant the heel of his hand in the man's face and shove him away.

Thankfully, the man ducked his head and hurried off.

Emma gave a short laugh and kept her face turned away. He guessed she sensed his disapproval. He hoped she put it down to talk of her being a nurse when the emotion that bit at his thoughts was far more elemental. He resented the freedom the man and so many others seemed to have about touching Emma. He snagged Jessie as he prepared to run after a friend. "Let's go home."

Emma restricted her conversation to comments on the concert as they walked toward the boardinghouse, which suited Boothe just fine. He was in no mood to talk. As soon as they got home, he insisted Jessie prepare for bed and followed him to their room.

"Is Miss Emma going to tuck me in tonight? Like a mommy does."

"She isn't your mother yet." Boothe struggled to keep his words soft, but he

169

didn't want Jessie building too many dreams that were destined to be shattered. "She might not want to tuck you in even when she is."

"Yes, she will. She likes me a lot. I can tell."

Despite his own warring emotions, Boothe laughed. Oh to have the confidence of a six-year-old. He didn't leave the room after he smoothed the covers over Jessie. Instead, he lay on his bed, a lamp burning on the dresser. He wished he had something to read, but he normally spent only sleeping hours in this room.

"Daddy?"

"Yes?"

"Will we live here when we marry Emma?"

"I don't know. Aunt Ada will still need our help." He hadn't thought about it because it wasn't going to happen. Yet a picture flashed across his mind of Emma in the kitchen, children playing in the yard and — he closed his eyes and called himself every kind of stupid.

"I could stay here, and you can move upstairs with Mom — I mean, Miss Emma."

He wouldn't even allow his thoughts to take that journey. None of Jessie's wishes, nor any of Boothe's stupid dreams would be fulfilled. "I don't know if that would be a good idea."

"Why not?"

Boothe didn't want to discuss it. He didn't want to think what would happen after the court date. All that mattered was keeping Jessie. The rest he'd deal with on a need-to basis. "Go to sleep."

Jessie sighed and rolled over. In a few minutes he snored gently.

Boothe turned out the lamp. If only he could fall asleep as easily but he lay staring into the darkness for a long time.

This whole idea seemed reasonable in his frightened reaction to the lawyer's letter. But now he wondered how he would carry through without coming apart like a shoe with the stitching worn away. How would any of them?

The next morning, he hurried into the kitchen. He'd dismissed the troubling thoughts of last night. No reason he should concern himself with anything but his goal — to prove to the judge he intended to give Jessie a home equal to what Vera and Luke could provide. Perhaps not equal but adequate. It stuck in his craw to admit he couldn't give his son the best of everything, but he wasn't alone. The drought and

Depression had reduced many families to meager existence.

He had coffee made and bacon frying when Emma hurried into the room. He poured a cup of the brew as she secured her watch on the bib of her apron.

"Thanks." She took the cup and downed a mouthful. She must have burned her tongue, but she didn't seem to notice. "I'm late." She glanced at the clock and swallowed more hot coffee. "I don't have time for breakfast."

"You have to eat something if you're going to be on your feet all day. No judge will look favorably on a woman who got ill because she wouldn't take care of herself."

She jerked back as if he'd insulted her.

He ignored her stinging look, pulled out a chair and edged her toward it.

She resisted. "I'm not your responsibility because I agreed to a pretend engagement."

"How long does it take to eat a couple pieces of bacon? And I'll slice some bread for you." He figured he'd have some eggs fried by the time she'd managed that and persuade her to eat them, too.

She hesitated then sat down — rather begrudgingly he figured. "I'm going to be late."

He scooped out three slices of crisp bacon

and dropped them on her plate and quickly cracked two eggs into the hot fat, stirring them with a fork. He sliced two slabs of bread and slipped them to her plate. A minute later, he added the scrambled eggs.

She shot him a narrow-eyed look and ate hurriedly. She looked at the clock again, gasped and jerked to her feet. "I have to run. Thanks for the breakfast." She spared him an amused look. "And for making me really and truly late."

He grinned. "My pleasure."

And then she ran. Literally. He watched out the window as she trotted out of sight. Then humming, he turned back to breakfast. Most of the boarders had left for their respective homes to celebrate Christmas with their families, but Aunt Ada and Loretta would make an appearance any time now. A thought hit him hard enough that he gasped.

Christmas. Gifts. As Emma's fiancé, he would be expected to present her with a gift. What could he possibly get? He thought of the little bit of cash left from his first paycheck and the many incidentals he needed to buy. He could spare a bit for a present.

Jessie drifted into the room, rubbing his eyes.

"What are you doing up so early?"

"I want to see Miss Emma before she goes to work."

"You just missed her."

"Aww. Now I don't get to see her until this afternoon." Jessie gave a long, heart-wrenching sigh.

"She does have to work, you know."

"I know." He shot Boothe a quick look. "I bet she's the best nurse in the whole world."

"I wouldn't know." He didn't want to talk about that part of Emma's life. He didn't want to even think about it. There was no reason he should. After all, this was only temporary. "You can help me find a Christmas gift for her."

Jessie bounced up and down. "Goody, goody gumdrops. Can I buy something?"

"We'll choose something together." At Jessie's frown of disappointment, he added. "You can make her a card to go with it."

Jessie practically left skid marks on the floor as he raced back to their bedroom. He returned in a few minutes with a piece of paper and the package of crayons Vera had bought him. Another luxury Boothe could not afford. He clamped down hard on his teeth. Luxuries were nice, but the only thing Jessie truly needed was a warm and loving home and *that* he could provide.

174

"Maybe you should wait until you've had breakfast."

Jessie put his coloring things to one side and parked his hands on the table. "Okay. Where is it?"

Boothe laughed. He couldn't imagine life without his son. "You're quite the guy."

Jessie consumed his bacon and eggs so fast that Boothe blinked. "Might be a good idea to chew your food."

"I did." He shoved aside his plate. "I'm going to make a really pretty card with snowflakes and hearts." He shot Boothe a questioning look. "Can you draw kisses?"

How did you draw the way her lips felt cool beneath his? How did you describe the jolt of surprise at the sense of connection, the collision of something faintly dangerous? "I don't know."

Jessie kept busy with his card while Boothe took care of chores. They headed for the stores right after lunch.

"I want to get her a real pretty brooch to wear on her pink sweater. I think she's pretty in that sweater, don't you?" Jessie said.

"Uh-huh." He'd actually never noticed. He'd been too busy trying to ignore her.

"She likes pretty things."

Boothe laughed. "How do you know so

much about her?"

Jessie ducked his head. "I like looking at her."

Sensing his son's embarrassment, Boothe restrained his amusement.

"I'm glad you like her, too," Jessie whispered.

Thankfully they arrived at the store so Boothe didn't have to respond. "Here we are. Let's see what we can find." He led the way inside.

Jessie hurried to the display case featuring jewelry, hair doodads and the kind of stuff Boothe hadn't looked at since Alyse's death. Fact is, even before that he hadn't spent more than a minute or two examining such stuff. Alyse always knew exactly what she wanted, saving him the need of making such choices. He stared at the display, overwhelmed by the selection.

In one corner was a brooch with pink stones set in the shape of a spray of flowers. "I like that one."

Jessie stood on tiptoes and leaned over the glass case. "I can't see good enough."

Boothe signaled the woman behind the counter. She pulled out the brooch, nestled against white satin in a blue velvet case.

"Ohh, pretty," Jessie said.

"How much?" Boothe feared it would cost

more than he could afford.

The woman named a price that would require a good portion of what he had in his pocket.

"It's perfect, Daddy."

He couldn't disappoint his son and nodded. "We'll take it." He dug out the money and waited for the woman to wrap it in a piece of fancy paper.

Jessie skipped all the way home, so excited that he couldn't stop talking. "Do we have to wait until Christmas to give it to her?"

"It's only two more days. I think we should wait."

Back at the house, he allowed Jessie to hide the box under his bed.

"I can hardly wait. Every Christmas I am going to buy her something special."

Boothe wanted to warn Jessie not to build dreams around Emma, but he had to keep the truth to himself until Vera and Luke's adoption request no longer posed a threat.

Emma worked again Sunday.

Jessie managed to get up before she left. "I want you to stay home."

"I'll be back by supper time and we'll go to the church program together." She looked as eager for their outing as Jessie.

Boothe stilled the screams in the back of

his head warning him people were going to be hurt by this deception, but none of them had a choice if he was to keep Jessie — and he intended to do whatever it took to ensure he didn't lose his son.

Emma waited until Jessie skipped away to whisper to Boothe, "I can hardly wait to see how excited the children will be at the gifts we made."

Boothe realized this brought the spark of excitement to her eyes, not the idea of spending time together, pretending to be engaged. He wasn't disappointed. Not a bit.

By the time they sat in the church watching the children act out the Christmas story, Boothe had quieted both his worries and his wantings. He sat beside Emma, his arm draped across the back of the bench, his fingers touching her far shoulder — for all intents and purposes, a happily engaged couple. They had to maintain that appearance and convince every observer of that fact.

And he had to remember this was pretend.

The program ended amidst loud clapping.

Emma edged forward as Pastor Douglas and his wife moved toward the tree where the gifts were piled. She squeezed his hand — a gesture he took to be as natural as the bright smile she sent him. And not in the least about him.

She perched on the edge of the pew as the children filed up to receive gifts.

A boy of about four or five sat ahead of them, clinging to his mother's hand as he watched the proceedings.

"Go ahead," the mother whispered, "I'm sure there'll be something for you."

The boy hesitated. "For me?"

Emma leaned over. "There's something special just for you. Go see."

The brown-eyed child ducked his head then glanced toward the front where children eagerly took their gifts and hurried to their parents. Still the boy hesitated.

His mother urged him forward, and he made it as far as the aisle before he stopped. Boothe could smell his fear and uncertainty and half rose, intending to lead him forward.

His mother pushed gently at his back. "You want a present, don't you?"

Nodding, the boy stepped into the aisle and tiptoed to the front.

Mrs. Douglas placed a gift and a pair of mittens in his hands. The youngster raced back to his mother and sat with the package in his lap, staring in wide-eyed wonder.

"Open it, dear."

Slowly as if wanting the moment to last

forever, he pulled off the wrappings to reveal one of the airplanes Boothe had made. Boothe knew a special bubble of happiness with the way the propeller spun on this particular one.

The boy flicked the propeller. "It really works," the boy whispered. "It really works."

Emma's eyes brimmed with pleasure as she hugged Boothe's arm and murmured in his ear, "You've made this child very happy."

Something wrenched inside him — a fragile sensation of hope that slipped past the barriers he'd erected and headed straight to a tender, eager spot in his heart. Anger followed quickly on its heels. This romantic setup was pretend. Temporary. She was a nurse. He had promised himself —

The eager light in her eyes faded. She pulled her hands to her lap and faced forward.

She'd taken his harsh expression as disapproval of her behavior. He didn't intend to tell her otherwise. They both needed to keep the boundaries firmly in place.

Jessie raced to join them. "Look at the great truck I got. I got to show Marvin." He took off as fast as he came.

People started to mill around, visiting neighbors, wishing each other a blessed

Christmas. Pastor and Mrs. Douglas made their way to Boothe and Emma.

"I want to thank you both for taking care of the gifts. Your generous deed has made many children happy," Mr. Douglas said.

"What's this I hear about you two?" Mrs. Douglas didn't wait for an answer. "Congratulations. You're perfectly suited to each other." She hugged both of them.

Boothe resisted an urge to argue. The Douglases hardly knew him. They weren't aware of his doubts about God's love and faithfulness. Nor did they know he'd vowed to never forgive Alyse's death. His unforgivingness blanketed every nurse and doctor. He glanced at Emma's glowing face. Maybe she could switch to being a teacher. Or stop work altogether despite her insistence her family depended on her. Realizing his thoughts had gone to impossible territory, Boothe clamped his jaws into a locked position.

The Douglases moved away and another couple came to them — a pretty young woman and a man with Indian blood.

The young woman squealed and hugged Emma long and hard. "What did I tell you at my wedding? I said you'd be married before the year was out." She studied Boothe. "So you're the lucky man who has convinced Emma to let a little love in her life?"

Her words stung his heart like icy water. He was not a lucky man. He was a fake, letting people think he'd won Emma's love. "Fortunate the man who wins Emma's love."

Emma shot him a red-faced scowl then turned her smile to the others. "Charlotte, Kody this is Boothe Wallace. Boothe, the Douglases — Kody and Charlotte. Kody is Pastor and Mrs. Douglas's son."

They shook hands all around.

Charlotte hugged Emma again. "I'm so happy for you. If you know half the joy I've known with Kody —"

Kody grinned at her. "Doesn't take much to make you happy, does it?"

Chuckling, Charlotte cupped his cheek with her hand and gave him a look of pure adoration. "Only you."

"Ahem," Emma said. "We're still here."

"I haven't forgotten." Charlotte turned back. "I'm going to give a party to celebrate your engagement. How about New Year's Eve? Can you come to the ranch?"

Emma glanced at Boothe, her eyes questioning, full of regret and warning.

He shrugged. It would seem unnatural if they refused. "We'll be there."

Jessie hurried to them. "That was the best church Christmas ever. A real baby in the manger." The girl who played Mary had been allowed to bring her baby brother. "I been thinking —" He tipped his head and studied his father as if measuring him for some task. "Can we have a Christmas baby next year? Just like the baby Jesus?"

Kody choked back a laugh.

Charlotte sputtered.

Emma looked ready to melt like hot butter and slip through the floorboards.

Boothe grabbed Jessie's shoulder and turned him to face the younger Douglases. "Folks, this is my son, Jessie. Jessie, say hello to Mr. and Mrs. Douglas."

"Hello." He squirmed around to look first at Emma then Boothe. "Well? Can we?"

Boothe groaned. "We'll be sure to let you know."

Jessie nodded, his face so eager it rivaled the overhead lights. "I think God will send us a baby just like he sent baby Jesus."

At that moment, the building shuddered under a blast of wind. The bell in the tower overhead began to peal.

"Merry Christmas," Mr. Douglas called. "Now excuse me while I go secure the bell rope."

The first people to leave the building

called back, "It's snowing heavily." At their words, everyone gathered their things and headed for the door.

Boothe helped Emma with her coat and pulled a scarf around Jessie's neck. The wind attacked them as they stepped outside. Snow descended like a furry blanket. He grabbed Emma in one hand and Jessie in the other. "Hold tight." They'd have to face the wind for the walk home.

Away from the shelter of the church, the wind increased in fury. Emma stumbled. He held on and pulled her closer. She pressed to his side filling him with sweet delight at her unspoken trust. By the time they burst through the door into the warmth of the house, they puffed from the effort of facing the wind.

Jessie shed his coat and raced into the front room to show Aunt Ada his gift. Boothe hoped he wouldn't add his request for a Christmas baby.

Boothe hung his coat then saw Emma struggled to undo the scarf at her neck. Ice held the knot. He helped her. His fingers brushed her cold chin sending spears of unfamiliar sharpness coursing along his nerves. He stilled his fingers. Tried to quiet the sensation.

She pulled off the scarf and draped it over

a hook. She kept her back to him as she unbuttoned her coat.

He didn't move away but waited and held her coat as she pulled out her arms.

She turned. The word *thanks* froze to her lips as she met his eyes, correctly reading the wishing, the longing he couldn't deny.

He brushed moisture from her face where snow melted. Her skin flushed with exuberant color. Her eyes shone as if lit from within. Her mouth looked pink and kissable.

He bent his head and gently, tentatively brushed her lips. In the back of his mind, he remembered his decision to avoid kissing her again. But as her lips warmed to his, a great hand seemed to reach into his chest and squeeze his heart open, pouring in a warmth that healed wounds left by the loss of Alyse, smoothed lumps left by his anger toward the bungling nurse and doctor.

That memory served to set him back on his heels. He was only confusing gratitude at Emma's willingness to help him for something else — an emotion he wouldn't name.

He headed for the front room, murmured a greeting to Aunt Ada and Loretta as he crossed to the window and looked out at the snow. He felt, as much as heard, Emma follow him into the room. "This snow could be the break in the drought," he said in an attempt to put his thoughts back on practical things.

"It might have waited another day or two." Emma sound faintly amused. "Until I made my trip home and back safely."

He jerked around. "You're going home?"

She quirked one eyebrow. "For Christmas. I did mention it."

He vaguely remembered. But that was before —

Before they became engaged. Even if it was just pretend, he suddenly felt responsible for her safety. And how could he keep her safe if she went away?

"You're going to see your mommy and daddy?" Jessie's voice rounded with awe and surprise.

"Yes, I am. And my brother. I haven't been home in almost two months, and I miss my family."

"When you and Daddy get married, they'll be my grandma and grandpa, won't they? And my uncle?" Jessie quivered with anticipation.

Emma shot Boothe a desperate look. He read her silent challenge to extricate them from this.

"Daddy, can we go with Miss Emma?"

Jessie practically glowed. "To see my new grandma and grandpa and uncle?"

"Jessie —" His son built such high hopes on this little deception.

"I have to leave very early tomorrow," Emma said softly. "You'll still be sleeping."

"I can wake up. You'll see."

Aunt Ada put down her knitting and considered them. "It sounds like an excellent plan. I would feel better if Emma didn't have to travel alone."

"Emma travels alone all the time." Emma's mouth pursed as she spoke.

Aunt Ada nodded. "And I don't like it one bit. In my day —" She sighed. "Never mind. But shouldn't you take this opportunity to introduce Boothe and Jessie to your parents? They'll be anxious to meet them after they learn of your engagement."

Boothe didn't have to be much brighter than a five-watt bulb to understand Emma didn't welcome the idea. Certainly she might be reluctant to take this little deception of theirs any further. But it seemed there was something about her family she didn't want him to know. Or was it a convenient excuse for refusing to marry him? Not that he hoped to convince her to turn this pretend engagement into a real one. He managed to ignore the way his heart kicked with hope. No. They both had their personal reasons why it wasn't possible.

He faced Emma, a challenge burning on his face. "There's no reason we can't go, unless you don't want us to."

CHAPTER TEN

Panic flooded through Emma like the torrents of water that normally — before the drought — followed a spring thaw. It cornered her like a feral animal.

She could refuse but if she did — she looked at Jessie, so innocent and eager and then shifted her gaze to Ada — people would have reason to doubt the truth of their so-called engagement.

Boothe watched with mocking eyes, knowing she was well and truly trapped. She would do what she must to help Boothe — for Jessie's sake — but the look she flung Boothe was loaded with fire. She hoped it burned his conscience. "Of course, you're welcome to come with me."

His unrepentant grin showed no trace of the guilty regret she hoped for.

She sent a desperate prayer heavenward. *Lord, tomorrow would be a real good time for Jessie to refuse to crawl from his bed.* Everyone in the house knew Jessie was not an eager riser.

But at five thirty the next morning, they waited for her at the bottom of the stairs. Jessie yawned hugely but showed no sign of changing his mind.

"You should have stayed in bed." She spoke kindly to Jessie, but her eyes flashed her true feelings to Boothe. She didn't want him accompanying her and would not pretend otherwise.

He grinned. "I'm anxious to meet your parents."

"I'm sure." She had no idea what he really wanted, but seeing as their engagement was a mockery, and they would never marry, she couldn't imagine what perverse pleasure he got from this.

He took her bag, and they stepped out into cold so crisp that ice crystals stung her cheeks. She bent her head and was thankful the need to hurry to the station prevented her from facing what lay ahead.

They found seats in the train. Jessie insisted on sitting beside Emma, which left her little choice but to face Boothe for the duration of the trip. She shifted to stare out the window. The station agent pushed open a door to the platform. A square of light dropped to the wooden planks as he shoved the trolley inside. The conductor swung a lantern and hollered, "All aboard." The whistle blew and the train huffed from the station. Then her window became a mirror reflecting Boothe's face. He studied her. Something unfamiliar, frightening, yet teasingly warm, ticked behind her eyes. A nameless feeling she'd tried uselessly to deny since she'd first laid eyes on this annoying man.

She sent him a fierce look, but he'd already proved impervious to her annoyance. All he did was flash her another grin, which made her want to scream.

Jessie curled up beside her, his head on her knee. In minutes he snored softly.

Boothe chuckled. "The boy does not like giving up his sleep."

"You should have left him in bed." Now that Jessie wouldn't hear them, she intended to give Boothe the full brunt of her displeasure.

"He'd never forgive me if I went without him."

"You know that's not what I meant." She scrubbed her lips together. She felt a need to squirm but didn't care to disturb Jessie. Instead she rubbed her hands up and down her arms. She didn't want Boothe to meet her family.

He leaned forward. "What's bothering you? It seems perfectly normal for me to be introduced to your family. But you act like —" He shook his head. "Are they criminals or something?"

She gave him a long, hard stare. He would know the truth as soon as he met them. She might as well prepare him. "No, not criminals but —" The breath she drew in seemed to turn into a vacuum that left her struggling to fill her lungs. "It's my brother, Sid."

"He's a criminal?" He shot a look at Jessie. "He's not a risk to my son, is he?"

Emma blinked. She hadn't considered the idea but with Sid one could never quite predict. "I shouldn't think so."

He read the doubt in her voice. "You should have told me before we started. I'd never put Jessie in any sort of danger."

"I noticed how quick you were to hear my protests."

He let his shoulders relax. "You got me there."

"I have to tell you about Sid." Where to begin? How to tell him without revealing her deepest, darkest secret?

"Yes?" His voice indicated he wanted the truth.

She tried to create a condensed version of it. "Sid used to be a strong young man. You might even say daring and adventuresome. But he had an accident that —" She shuddered, felt her eyes go bleak. She'd never be able to remember that day without wanting to cry. She waited for the pain to pass, waited for it to suck out her insides, waited for the empty, dead feeling that would follow.

Boothe grabbed her hands as she scrubbed them up and down her arms. He curled them beneath his palm, calming their restlessness. "It's okay. I'm here. I'll walk with you through whatever it is."

She clung to his words as desperately as she clung to his gaze. "Sid has permanent damage from his accident." She breathed hard, couldn't go on. Her beautiful younger brother on whom her parents had pinned all their hopes — whom she loved like no other. "He hurt his head, and now he's like a child in his reasoning. He's fearful. Mother and Father have to watch him constantly. He can't be left alone." Her voice dropped to a whisper that caught on every word. "It's been very hard for everyone."

Boothe squeezed her hands. "Your parents expect you to look after them the rest of your life?"

She sat up straight. "No, I expect it of myself."

"Why?"

The look of pity on his face, as if she were only an overly emotional, silly-headed woman sent a bolt of anger through her. "Because I am to blame." She gasped and sat back. She had to make him believe she didn't mean it. "No, forget I said that."

He released her hands, leaving her floundering like a blind, frightened animal. She would not let him guess it and tucked in her chin and faced him with her best don't-mess-with-Nurse Spencer look.

"I have no intention of forgetting such a statement. Why should you blame yourself? Didn't you say it was an accident?"

Pliers would not open her mouth. Not even her best friend, Charlotte, knew her secret.

"Seems like an awful weight to carry around the rest of your life."

They stared at each other like adversaries in a boxing ring.

"Accidents happen. A person should forgive and move forward. Without assigning blame."

She snorted. "This from a man who blames a doctor and nurse for an accident. Seems you should follow your own advice before you expect anyone else to."

His expression underwent a transformation from kind and pleading to an angry scowl drawing his eyebrows together and filling his eyes with darkness. "That was different."

"How?"

"They insisted on being right rather than admit their mistake."

"But it was accidental. One shouldn't assign blame. One should move on." Her voice held a mocking tone as she repeated his words.

His scowl intensified.

She lifted one shoulder in a half-hearted shrug. "Give me advice when you're ready to follow it yourself." She got no pleasure out of hurting him. She only did it to protect herself.

He crossed his arms over his chest and kept his gaze locked on something at the end of the car.

That suited her fine. She did not want to continue this conversation. She stared out the window, but glimpses of Boothe's reflection disturbed her efforts to ignore the man. She pulled a book from her bag and pretended to read even though the light was poor and she had no interest in the story.

An hour passed in silence. They would soon arrive in Banner. Before they did, she must extract a promise from him. "Please don't say anything about this to my parents."

"This? You mean our engagement?"

"No. I mean what I said about Sid."

"I'm sure they already know he had an accident." His voice was dry as toast.

Was he being purposely obtuse, or only trying to force her into saying more than she wanted? Which, she could tell him, would not happen. She'd kept her secret eight years. By now she was an expert at it. "About it being my fault."

She ducked her head to avoid seeing how his look overflowed with disbelief. She felt his silent waiting like a blast of overheated damp air sucking at her lungs.

"They don't know you blame yourself?" His words, though barely above a whisper to avoid disturbing Jessie, rang inside her head like the clanging of a bell. "Isn't this something you should discuss with them?"

A protest exploded through her thoughts. "They don't know I'm to blame." She could never confess the truth. She'd promised Sid. Although he didn't seem to remember, she did. She'd never be able to forget. Or forgive herself.

Carefully avoiding Boothe's eyes, she pressed her nose to the window, cupping her hands around her face to block out the light. In the distance, a faint glow indicated the Banner rail station. "We're almost there. You should probably wake Jessie."

Only then did she allow herself to face Boothe.

He studied her intently. "Fine. Pretend there isn't a problem." His gaze flashed mocking amusement. "But I would have never guessed the practical, efficient, organized Miss Spencer would avoid confronting something."

His attitude irked her. "Mr. Wallace, when you deal with your ghosts, I'll consider letting you give me advice about mine."

His eyes glowed with some sort of victory as if he'd won the argument.

She realized he'd succeeded in getting her to say she had ghosts in her past, though they were only dark shadows she preferred to avoid.

Not bothering to disguise his grin, he slid forward and shook Jessie. "Time to wake up, son."

Jessie burrowed against her leg.

Boothe leaned closer.

She could smell the soap he'd used, the warm wool of his coat and something more she couldn't identify but would recognize anywhere as uniquely Boothe. She wished —

She closed her eyes as warring emotions rattled her composure. She was angry with this man for prodding her. It was his fault she was forced to pretend a lie with her parents and Sid.

Jessie mumbled a protest and clutched the fabric of her coat, reluctant to leave his sleep.

"Come on, Jessie. Time to wake up." Boothe shook him gently, then when Jessie continued to resist, Boothe slipped his arm under his son's shoulders and lifted him. The warm brush of his arm against her side poured such a longing into Emma that she strangled back a sob.

If only this engagement wasn't pretend. If only —

She slammed her mind against such thoughts. No more "if onlys."

The conductor came through the car, announcing, "Banner, next stop."

Sleep left Jessie in a clap of noise. "We're there?" He squirmed from Boothe's arms and scrambled to the window. "I don't see anything."

Emma laughed, glad to be diverted from the direction her thoughts seemed determined to go. "It's still dark, but once we're at the station there will be lights."

"Will your father or brother meet us?"

Jessie's words were muffled against the windowpane. His breath formed a frosty barrier that he scraped away.

"No. Mr. Boushee, the baggage man, will give us a ride to the farm." She leaned over, her shoulder against Jessie's, as eager as he for her first, familiar glimpse of Banner.

The train slowed. The shadowed platform came into sight and then a pool of light around Mr. Boushee as he waited for the train to stop.

"We're here." She struggled to get her gloves on and dropped her book as she tried to put it in her bag. What would Mother and Dad say about her guests? Her insides quaked. Was there any way to explain the situation without jeopardizing the very reason for the pretense?

Boothe caught her hands. "You're shaking."

She dismissed it with a tight laugh. "It's only the rattle from the train still going through me."

He raised his eyebrows. "Really?"

She nodded. "Don't you feel it?"

"No. What I feel is a young woman worried when she shouldn't be."

It was her turn to voice disbelief. "Really?" She could think of several very good reasons to worry about this meeting.

"Don't you think they'll understand when it's over and you explain?"

"I hope so." She sounded as unconvinced as she felt.

Jessie trotted down the aisle to wait at the door. Boothe and Emma followed more slowly. Boothe grabbed her arm to whisper, "This pretense is hard for me, too. But I'll do anything to make sure I keep Jessie. And you promised to help."

She met his hard look without flinching. "I haven't changed my mind." He'd cleared away all her confusion by reminding her neither of them had any special feelings toward the other.

She hated lying to herself because she'd had unwanted feelings from her first glimpse. She lifted her chin and faced the future.

Mr. Boushee eagerly agreed to give them a ride to the farm. "Just in time for Christmas. Your folks said you'd make it but when you didn't come in last night . . . Well, I supposed you might have been called to work." He turned to speak to Boothe and Jessie in the backseat. "We're mighty proud of our young Emma. A nurse in the big city and all."

Emma chuckled. Favor didn't qualify as a big city to many people.

Boothe grunted, a sound Emma took for annoyance or disbelief or both. She understood he didn't like being reminded she was a nurse.

Twenty minutes later, just as the sun flung pink ribbons in wild abandon across the eastern horizon and the snow turned into blue-shadowed drifts, they pulled up at the farm.

Dad flung open the door and waved.

Emma jerked from the car and raced toward him. She stopped short of throwing herself into his arms.

He leaned heavily on his cane and smiled. "Welcome home, daughter." She knew by the way he stood that his arthritis had grown worse since she'd last visited. A giant ache filled her. He'd counted on Sid's help from the time her brother was old enough to carry a bucket or wield a pitchfork. Now he struggled through the work on his own, managing around his pain.

"Glad to be here." It had always been the same between them. This strain or awkwardness or whatever it was. A one-sided longing on her part for more. But more what? Her father wasn't a warm, affectionate man, but she knew he cared for her.

Mother called from the kitchen. "Come inside before we freeze. I'll have breakfast ready in two shakes."

Mr. Boushee carried her bags to the step and suddenly she remembered Boothe and Jessie. "I brought company."

Dad called over his shoulder. "Mother, she's brought company."

Mother hurried to the door wiping her hands on her apron.

Emma waved for Boothe and Jessie to join them. "Mother, Dad, this is —" She'd thought of a hundred different ways to introduce Boothe and explain their relationship. None of them seemed right. "Boothe Wallace and his son, Jessie."

Boothe shook hands with them both. An awkward silence hung like a transparent curtain. She felt her parents' silent questions, Boothe's patient waiting. But she didn't know what to say.

"My dad and Miss Emma are 'gaged. You're going to be my new grandma and grandpa."

No one spoke. Jessie glanced back at Boothe. "Isn't that right, Daddy?"

Boothe cupped Jessie's shoulder with his big hand. "That's right." He draped an arm around Emma's shoulders and smiled down at her. "You have a lovely daughter."

Emma couldn't speak as her insides twisted with anger. This was carrying the deception a bit far in her opinion.

Emma's dad broke the strain first. He held out his hand to Boothe. "I hope you're a good man. Our Emma deserves no less."

"I'll always treat her the very best," Boothe assured the older man.

"Well, come in, come in." Mother shooed them inside.

Sid waited for her beside the stove, poised, ready to run if something frightened him.

Emma paused, signaling Boothe and Jessie to wait, and stepped forward so Sid saw no one but her. Her insides welled up. As handsome as ever, grown tall and filled out into a good-looking man, his thatch of blond hair shining, his blue eyes overly bright with things she couldn't understand, sometimes fear, other times excitement. This morning she hoped it was the latter. She held out her arms. "Hi, Sid. How about a hug?"

He flung himself into her embrace. She backed up to keep from toppling. "Emma, Emma, Emma." He said her name over and over in an endless word. "Emmaemmaemma."

She eased out of his grasp. "I have some friends for you to meet." She took his hand and pulled him forward.

Sid started to roll his head from side to side. He clutched her hand so hard that she had to wriggle her fingers. A low moaning sound escaped his mouth.

"Sid. They're my friends. They won't hurt you."

Boothe waited for Sid to accept his presence, but Jessie raced forward and touched Sid's arm. "I'm Jessie and you're going to be my uncle, Sid."

Sid stiffened. Dad guarded the door. Mother made shushing noises that sometimes calmed Sid. Boothe reached for Jessie. "Son, take it easy. Give the man a chance —"

"Uncle Sid." Sid's words rounded with awe. "Me, Uncle Sid." He reached for Jessie's hand. "Me, Uncle Sid. You call me Uncle Sid. Okay?"

Jessie nodded, grinning from ear to ear.

The whole room seemed to sigh. Another crisis averted.

"I show you my rocks," Sid said to Jessie.

Emma touched Sid's shoulder. "Wait. I want you to say hello to Boothe Wallace, Jessie's father. He and I —"

Sid didn't let her finish, saved her the necessity of trying to explain the relationship. "Hi, Boothe Wallace, Jessie's father." He beamed at Jessie. "You see my rocks?"

"Sure."

Sid kept his box of treasures in the corner

of the kitchen farthest from the windows, and he led Jessie there. Emma and her parents had never been able to understand Sid's fascination with rocks but he sat cross-legged on the floor, Jessie beside him, and they soon engaged in a nonstop conversation about his collection while Mother made breakfast.

In a few minutes, they gathered around the table. Sid consented to join them when Jessie led the way. He sat beside Mother and insisted Emma sit on the other side. He eyed Boothe but ducked away whenever Boothe looked in his direction.

Emma sent Boothe an apologetic glance. He gave her a warm, understanding smile.

Sid noticed. "You like my sister."

Boothe nodded.

Sid turned to Emma. "You gonna marry him? Like Mom and Dad?"

"That's what it would be like." *If we married,* she added silently.

"You like him a lot?"

She couldn't meet Boothe's eyes, couldn't look at her parents. How could she answer honestly? She didn't want to confess she liked him in front of all these witnesses. Finally, she found the right answer. "He's a good man."

Sid nodded his approval then turned to

his food.

After breakfast while Emma and her mother cleaned up the kitchen, Father headed out to finish the chores. Boothe volunteered to help.

Seeing Sid playing on the floor with Jessie while Father limped out to cope with work Sid should have done, Emma struggled to keep her sorrow buried. If only Sid wasn't afraid to go outside, he could still help, but the moment he saw the open spaces he started to run. One time Emma chased him for an hour before she succeeded in turning him around.

"That's the happiest I've seen him in a long time," Mother said, watching Sid and Jessie play together.

Emma nodded and smiled. Yes, it was nice to see him enjoying himself, but he was playing with a six-year-old. How happy could she be about that? Her brother, who had been big and bold and beautiful. He was still big and beautiful. She'd trade them both for bold and normal.

Boothe and Dad returned with Boothe carrying the bucket of milk and three eggs. Emma hoped he'd found them before they froze.

" 'Preciate your help," Dad said, deepening the ache in Emma that went on and on like the prairie sky.

As soon as the milk was strained and put to cool and the chicken was baking in the oven, Mother shooed them into the front room to open gifts.

Emma took things from her overnight bag before she joined them. She'd bought yard goods for Mother, warm mittens for Dad and a small wooden box with a lid for Sid. He opened it and saw the tiny glistening rocks she'd gathered for him on a trip into the hills to visit Charlotte and Kody.

"Ohh, this is nice." He pulled out each of the dozen stones and passed them around for inspection.

When he finished, Emma opened her gifts from Mother and Dad. Dad had built a small tray for her stationery and Mother had crocheted a lace doily. "Thank you so much."

She handed out the gifts she'd brought with her for Boothe and Jessie. She bought them Saturday and thought she'd leave them on the kitchen table for them to discover after she left. That was before she'd been hornswoggled into letting them accompany her.

"How —" Boothe asked, staring from her to the gift.

She laughed, pleased beyond belief that

she'd surprised him.

Jessie opened his gift and showed a red rubber ball. "Thanks, Miss Emma."

"Can I play ball with you?" Sid asked, eyeing the ball with interest.

"Sure."

"Better wait until we finish." Boothe slowly, painstakingly untied his parcel. When he pulled out a pocket-sized whetstone, he grinned from ear to ear. "I couldn't have asked for anything better."

The look he gave filled her with a warmth that turned her insides into pudding.

Suddenly aware of how long they'd been staring at each other, she cleared her throat and jerked her unwilling gaze away.

He nudged Jessie, who vibrated with excitement. Jessie pulled a parcel from behind him and, his eyes glowing, handed her a prettily wrapped gift.

"How? When?"

He chuckled. "I love surprises, don't you?"

She nodded.

Jessie stood in front of her. "Open it. Hurry."

"Jessie," Boothe warned but Emma laughed.

"It's okay. I like his enthusiasm."

"It's good for us all to have a child around." Dad spoke with such weariness that Emma's pleasure in pleasing Boothe with her gift vanished like a snowflake on a hot stove. She knew how difficult it was for her parents to care for Sid, how their dreams had been shattered and all they had to look forward to was constant supervision.

She silently renewed her vow to help them the rest of her life.

She opened her gift. A little brooch like a spray of spring flowers. "It's lovely." She pinned it to the shoulder of her gray sweater. "Thank you."

Intending only to spare Boothe a quick glance, she found she couldn't look away from his dark gray gaze. She felt every beat of her heart against her ribs as she silently explored the fragile feelings between them.

"Jessie helped me choose it," Boothe said, breaking the spell.

Again she reminded herself of the reality of her situation — a pretend engagement, a never-ending responsibility.

"Well," Mother said, pushing to her feet. "I'll get busy on dinner."

"I'll help," Emma gratefully escaped into the kitchen leaving Boothe to visit her father while Sid and Jessie played with the red ball.

They ate a simple meal of roast chicken, mashed potatoes, turnips and pumpkin pie.

Then it was time to play table games. They played simple games that both Jessie and Sid could enjoy.

Emma's heart filled with grateful admiration at the way Boothe amused them. She would be sure to thank him for his kindness to Sid as soon as they were alone, which with some forethought on her part and any amount of cooperation from others, wouldn't be any time in the near future. She found it harder and harder to deny her feelings for him. And she must. She would play this pretend engagement out until the court proceedings, and then maybe she'd find a job elsewhere. Maybe closer to home so she could relieve her parents on her days off.

Bedtime approached. "Mother, I'll make up the extra bed." She grabbed sheets and headed for the small, unused room. Boothe and Jessie would be comfortable here, and if Dad kept the stove going all night long, they'd be warm enough.

When she returned to the kitchen, only Boothe and Jessie remained. Jessie's sprawled arms on the table cradled his head.

"Where is everyone?"

"Gone to bed."

"I have your room ready."

Boothe nodded. "Jessie is more than

ready." He scrubbed his hand across Jessie's head but his eyes remained locked with Emma's.

"Come. I'll show you." Her mouth said come but her heart said stay. Stay and talk. But what was there to talk about? They both knew this was only make-believe.

Jessie stirred. Boothe scooped him into his arms and Emma led the way to the bedroom. Jessie curled into a ball when Boothe put him down. A now familiar and unwelcome yearning churned up her throat like a squatter with the intention of staying.

"I need to get our bag." Boothe turned and bumped into Emma, who stood like a thoughtless statue in the doorway.

He narrowed his eyes as she stared at him.

Afraid he'd read things in her gaze she didn't want him to, she hastily backed away. He headed toward the kitchen where his bag sat under the coat hooks.

CHAPTER ELEVEN

"Daddy, look at the snowbanks. Can we go slide on them?" Jessie stared into the bright outdoors.

Boothe had helped Mr. Spencer with chores before breakfast and now sat at the table enjoying a second cup of coffee. "Sounds like fun."

Jessie raced to Sid's side where he sat playing with his rocks. "You want to come out and play, Uncle Sid?"

Sid shrank back. "Don't like outside."

Emma signaled Jessie to her side. "Sid's afraid of outside."

Jessie looked shocked. "Why? It's fun."

Aah, Boothe thought. *That explained why Sid didn't help with the chores. Despite his mental limitations, Sid was a big man. He ought to be able to do a hundred things Mr. Spencer struggled with.*

Jessie returned to Sid's side. "Won't you

come and play with me?" He held out his hand.

Sid studied the extended hand, turned his gaze upward to Jessie's smiling face. He scrambled to his feet. Beaming, he announced. "I'm going to play with Jessie. He's my friend."

Boothe felt a collective drawing in of breath as the pair headed for the door. Sid pulled on a heavy coat, overshoes, hat and mittens just as Jessie did.

Emma rushed for her own outerwear. "I'll watch him."

Mr. Spencer pushed to his feet. "I'll be right along."

Whatever they seemed to expect to happen, Boothe intended to be part of if only to make sure Jessie was safe so he grabbed his coat and boots.

The sun shone bright enough to hurt his eyes. He pulled his hat lower to provide shade.

Jessie spied the sleigh Mr. Spencer used to trundle things back and forth between the house and the barn and grabbed it. "Let's slide down the hills."

Sid nodded, his eyes locked on Jessie's movements.

Emma hovered like a mother bird.

Banks of soil drifted against fences and

buildings created hills, now dusted with snow. It seemed symbolic of the whole place — Emma's parents, weary and worn, hiding it behind a dust of a smile. Even Emma looked older here.

Sid followed Jessie to the top of the first hill. He looked around him. An expression of pure, uncontrollable panic swathed his face.

"Sid," Emma called. "Sid, look at me." She raced after him so suddenly, Boothe could only stare.

Sid shuddered and started to run.

Emma scrambled up the hill. "Sid. Sid."

Boothe broke into a desperate run though he wasn't sure why. He only knew Emma sounded frantic.

Sid slipped on the snow and stumbled, gained his feet and continued on.

Emma reached him, grabbed his arm. "Sid. Stop. Come on. Let's go inside."

Sid dragged her after him. A sound like the sighing, crying wind, came from his throat.

"Emma, stop him," Mr. Spencer called from the door as he tried to make headway with his crippled gait, hindered by his need to lean on the cane.

Boothe didn't know what sent them all into such a panic, but Emma continued, unsuccessfully, to try and stop Sid. He reached the pair. "Sid, Emma's trying to tell you something." When he realized Sid wasn't about to slow down, Boothe grabbed his arm and wrenched him to a halt.

Emma flashed a look of gratitude. "Sid, let's go home. See. Dad's waiting for you."

Boothe turned Sid toward the house.

They got through the door and helped Sid to a chair. Emma bent to remove his overshoes.

Jessie, eyes wide, followed. He faced Sid. "What's wrong? Why did you run?"

Sid shielded his eyes. "I don't like the open."

"Then don't look."

Sid dropped his hand and stared at Jessie. "That's right. I shouldn't look."

Emma chuckled. "There you go, Sid. Just don't look."

But no one suggested Sid go outside again, and after a bit, they had lunch of stew made from the leftover chicken.

Sid let Jessie sort through his rocks but carefully arranged them into orderly rows after Jessie set them aside.

It was a shame. Sid was tidy, well-behaved, gentle and kind — traits that would serve him well if he had a job somewhere. A man didn't have to work outside. Boothe himself was evidence of that. He worked in a garage. Yeah, he walked back and forth, which might present a problem for Sid. But still. There had to be something he could do. How long would Mr. Spencer be able to keep up with the farm work? He could barely walk. Emma should not feel she had the sole responsibility of supporting the family. He couldn't imagine why she blamed herself for Sid's condition. Accidents happened. He refused to give Emma's comments about Alyse's death any credit. *Her* death wasn't simply an accident.

"Your turn," Emma said. They played a game of chicken foot with dominoes. To him it was a simple game but she seemed to figure strategy was involved and took her time assessing all options.

Mrs. Spencer had announced she intended to nap after lunch, and Mr. Spencer nodded in the rocking chair.

The game over, Emma jumped up. "I have a treat." She hurried into her bedroom and returned with a small sack she handed to Sid. "Share with everyone."

Sid opened the sack and looked in. "Ooh." He pulled out an orange and handed it to Jessie. He carefully placed one in front of Boothe. He thanked Emma as he placed one in her hands. "Two left. One for

Mother. One for Father."

Mr. Spencer stirred and Boothe took him an orange.

Mother hustled into the room. "I must get supper ready." But she took the fruit Sid offered and sat at the table to peel it.

"I'll make tea," Emma offered and supper was momentarily forgotten as the four of them drank tea and visited. Boothe felt Emma's look of appreciation when he regaled them with stories of activities at the boardinghouse. They seemed especially eager to hear about Emma's part in planning the Christmas gifts for the children.

They hurried through supper. At seven, Mr. Boushee arrived, as arranged, to pick them up.

"Come on, Jessie," Boothe called. "It's time to go."

"I won't forget," Sid said, as Jessie turned to obey his father.

Boothe waited until they were in the train to ask Jessie about what he'd said.

Jessie studied his hands. "I told him I knew about being scared. I told him something I remember. 'The Lord is my shepherd.' " He fixed Boothe with a determined look. "I think it means God takes care of us and 'tects us."

Boothe's thoughts stung with remembrance. Alyse had taught Jessie the verse. He'd mocked her, saying the boy was too young and the words meant nothing to him. How wrong he'd been. He stared down the tunnel of his memory. How many other times had he been wrong and didn't know it?

At the gentle concern in Emma's eyes, he realized his expression revealed far more than he wanted. He turned back to Jessie. "I think you're right, and it was wise of you to tell Sid."

Jessie bounced to the edge of the worn leather seat. "I like Uncle Sid. When can we visit him again?"

"I don't know." Every day this plan of his gathered momentum, collecting bits and pieces of future sorrow. He couldn't meet Emma's eyes, fearing her silent accusation.

Jessie spoke. "Sid gave me this rock so I won't forget him. I told him I don't need a rock. I will always remember him. I didn't have anything to give him. Maybe I can send him something."

"That would be nice."

"I like the farm." Jessie continued to talk about his experience for the rest of the trip.

Emma seemed preoccupied. Boothe missed the fun she'd been on the trip to Banner — feisty and kissable.

Whoa. Kissing is over. This relationship was business. Nothing more. As it was, far too many people stood to be hurt, but he didn't know what else he could do. Except keep things as businesslike as possible.

Only six more weeks and the court date would arrive. Until then all he had to do was go to work, come home and spend a couple of unbearably sweet hours in Emma's company.

But he'd forgotten the Douglases' invitation.

Emma pulled him aside the afternoon of the party. "I'll never convince Charlotte we're really engaged." She twisted her hands together and sounded thoroughly unhappy.

He wanted to still her hands, but since their trip to the farm, he'd found it increasingly hard to remember this was a pretend engagement and had done his best to avoid touching her or being alone with her.

She gave him a misery-filled look. "I can't stand the thought of Charlotte thinking I'm trying to pull the wool over her eyes."

He forgot all his reasons, all his warnings and squeezed her shoulders. "Emma, what would we have to do to convince her?"

She clung to his gaze, searching for his meaning. Her shoulders relaxed as she found the kindness he offered. "I don't know. How can we prove something that isn't true? I hate not being totally honest."

If he allowed himself total honesty, he would have to confess his growing interest in Emma — his enjoyment of her sweet nature, her manner of accepting life and dealing with it. He liked the way she cared about his son. He admired her easy grace and ready smile.

He slammed the door on such thoughts. That wasn't the sort of honesty she sought. From the beginning, she'd made it clear she had no room in her life for love and marriage. She'd been sure to remind him more than once since their visit to the farm. "You saw for yourself how my parents need help providing for themselves and Sid. He'll never be able to contribute. That leaves me."

He wanted to argue that it wasn't her responsibility, but how could he even suggest she abandon her concern? It wasn't that he didn't think she should help. But he resented how it left him with no hope. "What would you suggest we do differently?"

Her expression grew thoughtful. A flash of a smile widened her mouth.

His breath caught in the back of his throat as he waited expectantly for her answer.

But her shoulders drooped and her expression flattened. "I don't know."

Disappointment dug into his chest. She'd been thinking something more. He hoped she'd been about to admit she held some feelings for him. Perhaps even liked him a bit. Was it possible? "Emma, I think you are worrying too much what people will think." He spoke slowly trying to sort his thoughts ahead of his words. "Is it so hard to pretend we like each other?" He rubbed his knuckles along her jawline. She quivered beneath his touch. He hoped it meant she wasn't indifferent to him. "I don't have to pretend." His voice dropped to a husky whisper.

Her eyes darkened. He hoped she'd say she didn't have to pretend, either. But she stepped out of reach and lowered her head so he couldn't see her face. "It's not a matter of whether or not I like you. We both know this can only be pretend. Just until the court date. After that we have to tell everyone the truth. And for me the truth is . . . I can never contemplate marriage."

Did he detect a tremor in her voice? "I took you for a woman of deep faith. Isn't saying anything is impossible equivalent to saying God can do nothing?"

She jerked back and stared at him. " 'With God all things are possible.' I can't believe you're pointing me to faith. Have you allowed yourself to remember God's faithfulness?"

He gave a short laugh. "I long to believe as blindly as I once did. I don't suppose I ever will, though."

She smiled slowly. " 'With God all things are possible.' "

He didn't let his thoughts follow the trail of possibilities. "We can be friends without pretending, can't we?" He intended to get that confession from her mouth.

She nodded.

"That's all we have to do. For tonight, why don't you relax and have fun?"

She studied him. A mixture of doubt, dread and — dare he hope? — anticipation crossed her face and she smiled. "I suppose I could do that."

He felt as if he'd shed a heavy overcoat on a hot day.

And so they set out for the party in a car he borrowed from Mr. White. Jessie had been invited and bounced up and down in the backseat.

The stars shone brightly as they drove along the road. He wished they could keep driving until they reached a place where their troubles would disappear. Instead,

Emma pointed out the turn to the Douglases' home.

The ranch house surprised him — a large two-story log structure with lights flooding from top-to-bottom windows.

Charlotte and Kody stood in the open door. Emma rushed into her friend's arms.

Kody reached for Boothe's hand and shook it. "Welcome to our humble dwelling."

Boothe laughed at the gentle humor in Kody's voice. "It looks like a lovely home."

"The former owner built it. But we get to reap the enjoyment."

Charlotte drew Emma inside. Boothe and Jessie followed into the huge front room.

"I think you've met Star at church," Kody said to Jessie as he drew his daughter to his side. "She's five."

"Hello," Jessie mumbled.

Kody turned to the couple in the background. "These are my good friends, John and Morning." Kody's voice held a hint of caution as he introduced an Indian couple.

Boothe admired John with his proud stance and the gentle-voiced Morning. He liked Star immensely when she suggested Jessie might like to play.

"Not dolls," he firmly informed her. "I'm not playing with dolls."

Kody laughed as they marched toward the stairway. "They'll have fun together. Let me introduce Michael Barnes and his wife, Caroline. Michael is the town banker."

Boothe shook hands with the man he'd glimpsed in town. He appeared to be in his mid-thirties, his wife somewhat younger. It felt strange to be at a party with a banker who gave you permission to call him by his given name.

"I only wish the children could come, but Annie's been sick so we left her at home with her brother Henry," Caroline explained.

Charlotte allowed everyone to visit for a bit before she organized them into games. The children joined them for Blind Man's Bluff and Earth, Sky, Water. Star laughed so hard she couldn't speak let alone name an object from one of the elements. She giggled so hard Kody rolled his eyes, which sent Charlotte into peals of laughter.

Emma shook her head and chuckled. "I'd almost forgotten how much fun it is to be around all of you."

A fingertip of warmth trailed down Boothe's spine as he watched Emma relax and enjoy herself. As the evening passed, the tightness around her eyes left. She practically bounced with pleasure. Boothe had difficulty keeping his eyes off her. And to sit across the room watching her provided a lesson in self-control he didn't care to learn. He only wanted to go to her side and enjoy her presence.

Charlotte drew his attention from his useless wishing. "The children can bed down anytime. We have lots of room."

Boothe dragged his gaze from Emma's glowing face and noticed Jessie slumped in his chair. He knew a flash of guilt for not paying more attention to his flesh and blood instead of letting his mind wander along paths of never-to-happen delights.

"Come on, Jessie." He scooped his son into his arms and followed Charlotte up the sweeping staircase to a bedroom. Star hurried to another room without protest.

Back downstairs, Charlotte rubbed her hands in glee. "Now that the children are gone, we are going to celebrate a very special occasion — the engagement of my dearest friend, Emma, to this fine, upstanding man, Boothe."

The others clapped except for Emma, who shot him a help-me look.

Boothe smiled encouragement before he addressed Charlotte. "I might be a scoundrel, for all you know."

"Not if Emma has approved you. She's

not easily fooled. She's as practical as anyone I know. I mean, look at her. Have you ever seen her with her hair down?"

Boothe didn't turn his gaze to Emma. He didn't want to imagine anything about Emma above and beyond what he saw and dealt with every day. That was challenge enough.

"Have you?" Charlotte demanded.

He shook his head, still avoiding looking at the object of their discussion.

"She has waves of golden hair. If I had hair like hers, I would let it hang free. But not Emma." Charlotte gave her friend an affectionate smile. "She's careful about everything she does. She wouldn't fall in love with a man who is anything but good and fine and noble."

Emma made a choking sound, her face wreathed in merriment. "He's a regular saint all right."

Charlotte chuckled mockingly. "Well, maybe I overstate the facts but never mind. We want to celebrate with you."

Emma met Boothe's eyes and shrugged. He nodded. What could they do but go along with the whole thing? Not that he found it trying. Far from it. He ran his gaze over her hair and wondered what it would take to get her to free that golden glory from the combs.

Soon Charlotte stood before them, a piece of paper in her hands. "They haven't given us any particulars about how they met or when they fell in love. So I thought we'd fill in some of the details our way. I'm going to go around the circle and ask you each to give me words." She began with Caroline. "Name a day. It can be something special or memorable."

Caroline mused a moment. "The day it rained buckets."

Charlotte moved on, chuckling as she wrote down the words each supplied. "Now I am going to read to you the story of Emma and Boothe's romance." She cleared her throat and rattled her paper.

"Boothe, an *arrogant worm* from *Timbuktu* came to town *the day it rained buckets.* The first person he met was Emma, a kind but *bowlegged* young woman. Their first meeting occurred *long after midnight* while *the cat chased the birds.* He was impressed with her *purple* hair and *wooden* complexion."

By the time she finished, everyone laughed at the imaginary courtship of Emma and Boothe.

Emma wiped tears from her face. "That was great fun, Charlotte."

"I'll make a copy for you to keep."

Emma's expression turned wooden. "Thanks."

Boothe chuckled. "You can tell your grandchildren."

Charlotte waved a finger. "Whoops. Don't you mean *our* grandchildren?"

Boothe nodded. "Of course. A slip of the tongue."

Michael leaned over and whispered, "You'd better watch those slips of the tongue. Women are sensitive to those kinds of things." He squeezed his wife's hand and smiled at her. "Not that I mind."

Caroline widened her eyes and looked sufficiently surprised. "I don't recall you ever having such a problem."

Boothe watched the interplay between them, sweet with trust and familiarity. He missed having someone to share his thoughts with, who understood the things he didn't say. He and Alyse had shared something special, but he didn't ache for her as he once had. With a start, he realized it wasn't Alyse he wanted to fill the void. It was Emma.

Emma must have felt him twitch. "Are you okay?" she whispered.

He gathered up his thoughts and stuffed them into a strongbox, locked it and threw away the key. "I'm fine. I just have to be more careful about what I say."

Charlotte glanced at the clock. "It's almost midnight." She rushed from the room and returned with party hats and noisemakers to pass around. Kody went to her side as they all watched the clock.

"Ten, nine, eight —" They counted down together.

At midnight, they blew their noisemakers and shouted, "Happy New Year."

Kody and Charlotte turned and kissed.

Michael and Caroline turned and kissed.

Boothe turned and smiled down at Emma's cautious face. He knew he shouldn't kiss her again. But everyone would wonder if he didn't. He claimed her lips.

Kody hadn't lit fireworks. There were no flashing colored lights. Except inside Boothe's head.

CHAPTER TWELVE

Three weeks later Emma and Jessie walked along the sidewalk in front of the stores in Favor.

"Sid will really like what I sent him, won't he?" Jessie said.

Emma squeezed his hand. "He'll love getting a ball like yours."

Since the visit to her home, Jessie had a goal — he wanted to buy Sid a ball like the one Emma gave him for Christmas. He'd managed to earn the money on his own by running errands for the Millers next door and by sweeping the sidewalk in front of the general store. He finally earned enough to buy the ball, and they'd mailed it to Sid a few minutes ago.

"Sid will be so excited to get a parcel in the mail. I'm proud of you. You worked hard to buy his gift."

Jessie shoved his shoulders back. "Daddy says a person can always find work if they try hard enough."

Emma murmured agreement though she wondered where Sid fit into Boothe's philosophy. She might ask him except for one thing — since the party at Kody and Charlotte's three weeks ago, she'd done her best to avoid him. She'd taken extra hours at work. Said she had to visit former patients. Found a hundred reasons why she must rush over to Pastor and Mrs. Douglas's house to inquire about one thing or another.

She couldn't look at Boothe without remembering that New Year's kiss. It had not felt pretend. To her shame and embarrassment, she'd wrapped her arms around his waist, pressed her palms to his back and acted like she didn't ever want to let go. Only the laughter of the others forced her to back away. She hoped Boothe would take it as good playacting.

But she couldn't fool herself any longer.

She'd foolishly, hopelessly fallen in love. It wasn't something she was proud of.

It wasn't part of the bargain between them.

Only three more weeks until the court date and she'd put this whole awful, beautiful pretense behind her. She'd already started to look for jobs in North Dakota.

"When can we visit your farm again?"

Jessie asked.

"I —" She faltered. This was the hardest part of the whole deception — finding ways to answer questions from others without lying. "I don't know. It depends."

They had to pass White's garage on the way back to the house. Hoping to avoid seeing Boothe, Emma headed down the alley rather than pass the front of the garage.

"Can we go see Daddy?"

Emma hesitated beside the storage shed at the edge of the property. "He'll be working."

"I want to say hello."

A thump came from the building beside them. "Maybe that's him in the shed."

"Daddy," Jessie called. "Daddy, is that you?"

The world exploded in an angry roar and a flash so bright it seared the back of Emma's eyeballs. Flames erupted from the shed. The wall flew toward them.

Her heart kicked so hard it hurt her chest. She put out her hands to protect them. "Run," she screamed as the side of the shed slammed into her. "Jessie, run!" Hot air scalded her lungs. Heat seared her feet. She went down, the weight of the wall suffocating her. She fought to get oil-soaked air into her lungs.

She pawed at the weight pressing her to the ground. Panic, like a rabid animal, clawed at her.

"Jessie, where are you? Jessie!"

The weight on her shifted. She turned her head, her shoulders. She had to get up. She had to find Jessie. "Jessie!" She couldn't hear her own voice, only a roar like being run over by a train. She couldn't feel her feet. She twisted but couldn't see them. Panic clawed at her throat. *Where are my feet?*

"Jessie!" Her throat felt as if she'd swallowed rusty nails. Still she heard nothing.

She twisted and reached out, encountered a familiar texture. Jessie's coat. "Jessie, say something." Not a sound. Was he dead? Or was she deaf? She edged her hand over him, found his chest, felt it rise and fall. "Are you hurt?"

She edged her torso closer. Jessie's eyes were wide, blurred with confusion. He gave no indication if he saw her or heard her. Was she really speaking? She visually checked his head and neck for injuries then lowered her gaze.

Only her experience as a nurse kept her from crying out as she saw Jessie's exposed leg. The femur protruded. Blood gushed from the wound. Two thoughts twined through her mind. She had to stop the bleeding. The pain must be excruciating. "Jessie, be brave. I have to touch your leg."

She pressed down above the wound. The bleeding slowed and stopped. "Thank You, God," she whispered. She glanced around. They lay beneath part of the wall. Broken and splintered boards surrounded her. Fire licked at the edges. Panic seared her lungs. "Help. Help," she screamed, the words tearing from her throat. But she heard not a sound.

They had to get away. She pulled. Her legs would not move. With her free arm, she pushed at the debris. "Help! We need help!"

"Emma," Jessie moaned. "Are we going to die?"

His words came through mounds of cotton wool. She realized the explosion had rendered her temporarily deaf.

"Not if I can help it." She screamed again, ignoring the rawness of her throat. She was tempted to claw away the boards pinning them with both hands but if she didn't stanch the bleeding, Jessie would die. She could only bat helplessly with one arm.

"You aren't going to die."

Jessie clung to her gaze.

"I'll pray." She ached to help God but she was powerless. At His mercy. His tender mercy. She prayed out loud knowing Jessie needed to cling to faith as much as she. "Our Father, who art in heaven. Hallowed be Thy name." She said the entire Lord's Prayer. Never before had the words been more meaningful, or more comforting.

"Someone will find us." But they'd better come soon. She fell back as a black curtain crept toward the edges of her mind. *No. I can't pass out.* Jessie would bleed to death. She fought back the blackness and screamed again for help. She hoped it sounded louder to others than to her. *God, let someone hear me.* She glanced at the fire licking around the edges. They better hurry.

Boothe felt a shudder under his feet accompanied by a boom. He glanced up. They must be having trouble moving cars down at the rail yards. He bent over the engine he worked on.

"Boothe, fire." Mr. White grabbed buckets and headed for the back door.

A fire this close to the gasoline pumps . . .

Boothe dropped everything and ran. The storage shed at the back burned. One wall lay broken and shattered in the middle of the yard. Flames shot from the wall as well as the pile of debris that used to be the shed. Already half a dozen men organized a bucket brigade to tackle the fire. Others came on the run. Mr. Crukshank dug at the debris. What was wrong with the man? There was nothing worth saving. Putting out the fire was the first priority.

Boothe grabbed a bucket of water and threw it on the flames. "Where's the fire engine?" he demanded of the man next to him.

"On its way."

Mr. Crukshank yelled something. A ripple went up the line as they passed his message. One by one the men dropped their buckets and raced to Crukshank.

What was wrong with everyone? "Let's get this fire out," Boothe hollered.

"There's someone in there."

He dropped his bucket, soaking his trouser legs, and raced over. He grabbed a corner of the wall, along with five others.

"On the count of three," someone called. "And let's be careful. We don't know what —" He didn't finish as someone counted, "One, two, three."

Slowly the wall lifted. The far corner crumpled. They scrambled to prevent the wall from falling again.

Other men crawled over the debris. "Two of them," a disembodied voice called. "One of them's Nurse Spencer."

Another voice called, "The other's a kid and he's hurt bad."

The blood drained from Boothe's face, and his legs went numb. Black spots danced across his vision. Emma and Jessie. Buried in this mess. Jessie hurt. *God, forget all my doubts. Don't hold them against me at this time. Keep my son and Emma safe.*

The wall shuddered. Some instinctive voice warned him not to let go. If it fell —

"Take this," he hollered to a man racing to the scene. When the man steadied the wall, Boothe dropped to his hands and knees and headed into the mess.

Someone grabbed him. "Stay back, man."

"That's my son and my fiancée."

He saw Jessie. Saw the broken leg and the blood. He slithered closer. Fragments of broken wood grabbed at him, hindering his progress. Something sharp cut his palm. He ignored everything but his need to touch Jessie. Find Emma.

"He's alive," Crukshank said. "We have to get them out of here."

The heat of the encroaching fire brought beads of sweat to Boothe's forehead. He could see Jessie's face now. Even the ashes and dust couldn't hide his pallor.

Boothe shifted his gaze and stared into Emma's frightened, determined eyes. Several scratches marred her face. Was she okay? He scanned her body, praying she had escaped serious injury.

Her hands — his heart sank like a dead weight. Every beat brought pain. Her hands looked like raw meat. One lay across Jessie's leg. Gently, he reached out to lift it away.

"No," she screamed. "He's bleeding." She batted at him with her other hand.

He winced away.

He didn't want to further upset her, but he had to get both of them out of this mess before the fire spread. "It's okay. I'll take care of him."

She rocked her head back and forth. "No. You can't take care of him yourself. He must go to a doctor. I'll take him. I don't care what you think."

Nausea rose in Boothe's throat. His son was dying before his eyes. If they didn't move soon, they would all be burned, but the last time he'd taken a loved one to the doctor . . .

Emma turned to Crukshank. "Can you get us out together? And take us to the hospital."

"We'll do our best, ma'am." He turned and hollered. "Give us more room and send in a couple more men."

Boothe swallowed the bitter taste in his

mouth. "No need. I'll take Jessie." He tried to get his arms under his son, but Emma batted at him. He paid no attention. This was his son. He'd care for him.

Emma grabbed a shattered board and hit him across the side of his head. "I won't let you take him."

Boothe drew back. She'd surprised him more than hurt him.

He glowered at her. "He's my son."

"And you'd let him die before you'd go to the hospital."

Were her words slurred? He studied her more closely. Her eyes drifted shut. She jerked them open. She looked about ready to pass out any minute. But he didn't have time to wait for it.

"Boothe." Even his name dragged in slow tones. "Promise me you will take him to the doctor. If you don't, he'll die."

Boothe knew she was right. He'd seen the bone sticking out. He couldn't fix that.

Emma closed her eyes. "Boothe, it's time you let go of your blame and trusted someone." Her words were barely a whisper.

Could he trust anyone? Or maybe the question was, could others trust him to forget his anger and do what was right? What kind of man would put his son and fiancée at risk to prove himself right?

"Emma."

She cracked open one eye.

"I promise you I'll take you both to the hospital. You can trust me."

She looked deep into his gaze with barely focused eyes. Then she relaxed. "Thank you. See where my hand is? Slip yours under mine, and keep pressure there until you get to the doctor."

He followed her instructions. Felt the stickiness beneath his palm. "I've got it."

She fell back.

"She's passed out," Crukshank said. "Let's get out of here."

Someone helped Crukshank pull Emma from the debris. Hands reached out to guide Boothe from the rubble and into a car that whisked them away to the hospital.

Boothe never once let up the pressure on Jessie's leg.

God, help us. Please make both Jessie and Emma okay. Please, God. Please, God. He repeated the words nonstop.

"We're here," the man driving the car announced.

Dr. Phelps and a nurse raced for the car, pushing a stretcher.

Dr. Phelps opened the door and leaned in. "Good job. We'll take it from here." He put out his hand to replace Boothe's.

Boothe couldn't let go. He couldn't give his son over to this man.

Dr. Phelps turned his gaze to Boothe. "He'll be in good hands. I promise I'll care for him like he was my own son."

Boothe saw assurance in the doctor's eyes. Understood he could trust the man if he chose.

Boothe decided he would be the kind of man his loved ones could trust. He nodded and let the doctor put his hand over the bloody area. As soon as the nurse and doctor had Jessie on the stretcher, they raced inside and down the hall with Boothe on their heels. As he started to follow them through swinging doors, another nurse caught him.

"You can't go in there. That's the operating room."

Boothe swung around. "Where's Emma? I want to see her."

"She's having her burns looked at." She edged him toward a small room. "You wait here, and we'll let you know when you can see them."

He sank to the chair and bowed his head into his hands. *God, I never really stopped believing in You. You know that, don't You? I blamed doctors and nurses for Alyse's death. I blamed You. I wanted You to stop bad things*

241

from happening to me. A little selfish I admit. Now I know I have no right to ask anything of You. I don't deserve Your favor, but God, if You see fit, please let Emma and Jessie be okay.

Someone dropped a hand to his shoulder, and he looked up to see Pastor Douglas and his wife. "We've come to wait with you and pray."

"They can use all the prayers they can get. So can I."

The pair sat down beside him and bowed their heads. Betty slipped in. Then Aunt Ada. Slowly the room filled up with friends.

Boothe felt their care and support. Their spoken prayers sent encouragement to his fearful heart, but his ear was tuned for footsteps coming down the hall. Each time someone passed, his lungs forgot how to work.

He had no idea how long he waited. It seemed like eternity before the doctor stepped into the room. Boothe forced his rubbery body to stand and cross to the doctor.

Dr. Phelps smiled wearily.

Boothe's knees threatened to buckle. Did that smile mean bad news?

"Jessie is going to be okay. It's a miracle he didn't bleed out. You can thank Nurse

Spencer for saving his life. He'll be in traction for several weeks, but he ought to be as good as new once he's up and about."

Boothe shook the doctor's hand. "Thank you. What about Emma?"

"She still hasn't regained consciousness. It's a matter of wait and see. Her hands are badly burned. I've cleaned them up as best I can. They'll be bandaged while they heal." He chuckled. "I can't quite picture Nurse Spencer as a patient. I don't think she's going to be happy about being dependent on others."

"Can I see them?"

"Come along."

They entered the children's ward. Dr. Phelps pulled aside a dividing curtain between beds and ushered Boothe in.

Jessie lay on his back, his leg suspended from an overhead bar to a series of pulleys.

Boothe paused. It looked so barbaric. Was the doctor experimenting?

Dr. Phelps touched Boothe's arm. "It looks worse than it is. The weights on the pulleys keep the bone in alignment while it heals. Otherwise spasms will pull the bone crooked and he'll never walk properly again."

Boothe nodded. "Will Jessie be in any pain?"

"We'll do everything we can to make sure he isn't."

"How long?" Boothe waved at the ropes and pulleys.

"Could be as long as six months. But probably less."

Boothe couldn't speak past the lump in his throat. Jessie, who bounced from one activity to another, who never walked when he could run — he'd be confined like a trussed turkey for months. Boothe would help him. He'd do whatever it took to see his son well and strong again.

"He's still asleep from the anesthetic," Dr. Phelps said.

Boothe leaned over and kissed Jessie's forehead. "I'll be here for you, son. Whatever you need from me, I'll give." He straightened. "Where's Emma?"

Dr. Phelps signaled him to follow, and they crossed the hall into the women's ward. Again, the doctor parted a set of curtains.

Boothe hung back trying to prepare himself for the shock of seeing Emma helpless. He stepped forward.

She looked peaceful except for the huge bandages swaddling her hands.

"She won't be able to do a thing for herself."

Dr. Phelps nodded. "I suspect it will be

harder for her than many. She values her independence. She's got some damage to her lungs and throat from the smoke. She's still unconscious. There's a lump on the back of her head. But she's young and strong and stubborn."

"Can I stay with them?"

Dr. Phelps nodded. "They'll both be needing lots of help." He found a chair and parked it beside the bed.

Boothe waited until the doctor left before he bent over Emma studying her restful features. Her hair fanned out on the pillow as beautiful as Charlotte had said despite the smoke and debris in it. He tenderly stroked it back from her face. He leaned over and kissed the cut on her cheek. He would take her pain if he could. All he could do was be available for her. He whispered the same promise to her that he had to Jessie. "I'll be here for you, sweet Emma. Whatever you need from me, I'll give."

He jerked upright and crossed back to Jessie's bedside.

Pastor Douglas came in. "Boothe, we're here to help. What can we do?"

He wanted to be with each one as they wakened. He wanted them to see him when they opened their eyes and understand he would be there as long as they needed him.

But he couldn't be in two places at once. "If you could take turns sitting with one of them and let me know as soon as they stir . . ."

He couldn't say how long he waited. Hours ceased to exist. Time was measured by the next heartbeat and gentle breath of his loved ones.

"Boothe." Pastor Douglas touched his shoulder. "Jessie is waking up."

Boothe gave Emma a last lingering look. He'd been enjoying studying her peaceful features, filling his senses with the sight of her. He spun on his heel and hurried across the hall to bend over Jessie's bed. "Jessie, are you awake?"

Jessie's eyelids fluttered. He searched for the source of the sound.

"I'm here, son. I'm right here." Boothe's voice sounded as thick as it felt.

His son swallowed hard and whispered. "Daddy, I'm thirsty." He tried to sit. "I can't move." Panic gave his voice strength.

Boothe gently pressed him back to the pillow then held a cup with a spout to Jessie's mouth and let him drink. "You have a broken leg."

Jessie stared into Boothe's gaze, his look of fear and confusion tightened Boothe's ribs like a giant vise.

"We got hit by the shed. Emma caught the wall to keep it from hitting us. But it was too heavy." His eyes widened and he tried again to sit. Groaning, he fell back, panting as if he'd run three miles. "Where's Miss Emma?"

Boothe stroked Jessie's forehead. "She's in a bed across the hall. She's got burns on her hands."

"I want to see her."

"Perhaps later after you've both rested. Now you relax. I'll be here. If you need anything, you only have to tell me."

The breath went from Jessie's tiny chest in a whoosh, and then he dragged in more air. He closed his eyes. The covers rose and fell in steady rhythm. The nurse said, "He's sleeping. Rest is the best medicine. That and love."

"He'll get plenty of both," Boothe said.

He didn't want to leave his son even though he slept, but he needed to check on Emma, make sure she was okay and pray for her to regain consciousness.

Pastor Douglas nodded as Boothe returned to Emma's bedside. "She's peaceful."

Even unconscious Emma's faith felt alive and vibrant. Sitting at her side filled him with hope. Boothe hung his head. He didn't deserve one single bit of mercy from God, not after the way he'd pushed Him aside, blaming Him for everything that went wrong from Alyse's death to the drought, when all the time he could have chosen to trust God, to let Him hold his life in His all-powerful hands. Now when he needed God the most, he feared he had no right to ask for anything.

"I'll go sit with Jessie." Pastor Douglas squeezed Boothe's shoulder. "Remember, God is here for whatever you need."

I will never leave thee nor forsake thee. Great peace poured into Boothe's soul. God's faithfulness did not depend on Boothe but on His unchanging word. *Lord, whatever happens, I choose to trust You. Please, heal these two precious people.*

He lifted his head and stared into Emma's open eyes. Never had he seen anything more beautiful. He bolted to his feet and leaned over the bed.

"Emma. Welcome back." His words ached across his tongue.

A nurse hurried forward and took her pulse. Emma's eyes drifted shut.

"She'll probably drift in and out for a few hours."

Boothe waited a few minutes then returned to Jessie's room.

248

"How is she?" Pastor Douglas asked.

"She woke up for a few minutes."

"Praise God. A miracle for both of them."

"I don't deserve a miracle."

Pastor patted his shoulder. "None of us do. It is only by His great mercy that any of us receive blessings."

"I don't know if Emma is going to see this as a blessing." He chuckled. "I expect as soon as she's fully awake she'll be trying to devise ways she can manage on her own." He sobered. "This will not be easy on her."

Pastor Douglas agreed. "It's a good thing she has you."

Silently Boothe vowed she'd never regret having him if only for the duration of her wounds. A thought seared across his mind. Their pretend engagement would soon be over. They could have nothing more. She would never abandon her responsibility to her family. He wished there was some other way, but he respected her commitment. It was part and parcel of the strong, vibrant woman he —

Loved.

How could he be so foolish as to let himself fall in love with her? Yet he had. Helplessly, completely, joyously.

He vowed he would never utter a word of his love to her. He would not make this more difficult for either of them than it had to be.

CHAPTER THIRTEEN

The air sucked at her lungs, seared her eyes.

Sid. She had to get him out. She fought back the weight against her chest. Her hands wouldn't respond.

They were trapped. Sid. She had to save Sid.

Panic laced through her. She screamed and screamed.

"Emma." A voice whispered her name.

She turned, listened.

"Emma, you're safe. Wake up."

She struggled against the hand on her shoulder. Sid. She wanted to scream his name. The word formed in her mind but not on her lips. She tried to reach for him. Her hands refused to move.

"Emma, it's me. Boothe."

"Sid." She managed to croak his name. Wondered if anyone could hear.

"Emma. I'm here."

Boothe. He'd come. Her nightmare fled.

He'd help.

"Get Sid." Wait. It wasn't Sid; it was Jessie. Her panic shifted directions. Jessie had been trapped beside her. Bleeding. She struggled to reach him.

"Emma. Wake up. I'm right here."

The sound of Boothe's voice eased back her fear. Something cool swiped sweat from her heated brow.

The dream cleared. She opened her eyes and looked into gray calmness.

"Boothe?" she whispered.

"I'm here." He wiped her face with a damp cloth. "I'll be here as long as you need me."

She wanted to touch him, see if he was real or part of her dream. Her hands were so heavy. Pain scorched up her arms. She cried out.

"Oh, Emma. I wish I could take your pain for you."

She wished so, too. She closed her eyes and practiced the advice she so freely gave to patients. Deep breaths. Don't fight it. Ride the pain.

She wished someone had told her how futile such advice was. Then the pain eased marginally.

She met Boothe's gaze, sought the comfort he offered, and finding it, drew in a long steady breath that hurt all the way down. She moaned.

Boothe slipped his arm behind her shoulders and held a cup of water to her lips. "Drink."

She let each mouthful glide over her raw throat. Shouldn't it ease the parched feel? The fire. Of course. Her throat had been damaged.

She nodded to indicate she'd had enough to drink. Told herself she didn't want him to keep holding her, yet tears stung her eyes as he withdrew his arm.

Tenderly, he wiped them away. "I am so sorry."

She nodded. There was something she had to ask. She struggled to find the information in her mind. She closed her eyes, fought the bliss of sleep. It successfully claimed her.

Again, the terror of searching for someone and not finding him filled her sleep.

Boothe's voice wakened her. His touch on her forehead soothed her. His gray steady gaze and gentle smile calmed her.

"Jessie?"

"He's okay."

"Thank God." She swallowed hard. Tried to dismiss the torment dogging her thoughts. "It was so scary. I didn't want

Jessie to die. Or end up like Sid." She shuddered. "It was so much like Sid."

Boothe stroked her forehead. "It's all right now. Both of you are safe."

"No. You don't understand. I didn't stop him. I didn't help him." Her throat felt like each word was laced with razor blades, but she had to tell him all of it. Maybe then it would stop haunting her sleep. "We liked to play at the Holliday's farm. There were so few rules." She paused remembering it all. "Mother and Dad heard of some of the stuff like running down the barn roof and across the rickety lean-to. They forbid us to do it. But Sid —" Her voice caught.

Boothe held her shoulders and helped her drink more water. "You don't need to talk about this now. Wait until you're better."

"I have to tell someone."

He nodded. "I'm here if you need me."

She clung to his steady gaze. "Sid begged me not to tell our parents, and he and the Holliday boys raced off the lean-to into a stack of straw. The roof shook as they ran across it." She closed her eyes. Wished she could stop the memory. Knew it would never leave her. "They laughed. Thought it was fun. I wanted to stop Sid, but I didn't. I didn't want to ruin his fun. The roof collapsed. The Holliday boys managed to reach the straw stack but Sid — he fell. The space below was blown full of snow."

She tried to grab Boothe's arm, but for some reason her hands refused to move.

"He just plumb disappeared. I wanted to help dig him out but someone held me back. He wasn't breathing when they got him out. I didn't know what to do." She'd vowed she'd never again feel so helpless. When she became a nurse she'd learn how to handle emergencies.

Boothe didn't look away in horror and disappointment. Nor did he waste his breath trying to say it wasn't her fault. Because it was. She could have stopped Sid. She should have.

"Lie back and rest. Jessie is okay. He's across the hall with his leg in traction. You saved his life. Thank you." He pressed a kiss to her forehead.

She closed her eyes. She'd done something right. If only it would wipe away her guilt over failing Sid.

Light blared across her eyelids. She cracked them open. Sunlight flooded the room.

Emma glanced around. She was alone. And so thirsty her mouth felt like an acre of drought-stricken prairie. She reached for the glass of water on the bed table. Pain wrapped around her hands. They were mounds of white bandages. She remembered. They were burned.

"Boothe," she whispered. He'd been at her bedside every time she opened her eyes, but now he was gone.

She lay back and stared at the ceiling. *He's with Jessie, of course. Jessie's alive.* She remembered Boothe saying his leg was in traction. Thanking her for saving him and kissing her forehead in gratitude.

She smiled a little in spite of her pain. Boothe had sought the necessary medical care. He'd also promised to be here to help. Where was he? She needed a drink.

She remembered something else. She'd told him about Sid. Or was it only something in her dreams? No. She was certain she'd told him.

How would she ever face him? Even if he hid his condemnation, she could never look him in the face again without wondering what he thought. Though he could not accuse her more than she did herself.

Boothe stepped into the room. "Good morning. Nice to see you awake."

"It's not the first time. I seem to recall being awake off and on." Although she could barely speak past the dryness of her voice, she managed to express her annoyance. It defied reason, but she blamed him for knowing her secret.

He had the nerve to laugh. "Would you like a drink?"

She glared at him. Yes, she wanted a drink, but it about killed her to have to ask.

Still chuckling, he slipped his arm under her shoulders and held the glass to her lips. "I see you're feeling better."

She spared him a look full of annoyance and disbelief as she drank. "Thank you for the water. What makes you think I'm feeling better?"

"You're acting ornery."

Ornery? Not her. "I figure I'm being extremely patient considering the circumstances."

He laughed. Again. The man had a strange sense of humor. Something she hadn't noticed before. "Do you mind finding me a nurse?"

"What do you want? I can get it for you."

Her throat protested but her mocking laugh felt good. The dull redness that crept up his neck felt like justice.

"Oh. Of course." He rushed from the room.

Nurse Lang came in a few minutes later. "Needing some help?"

"I hate to bother you but with these —"

She held up her club-like hands.

"It's no bother to me. You call out whenever you need something." Lang helped her with her morning needs. "Breakfast will be here in a minute."

"Goody." As if she could eat breakfast with two worthless hands. "How bad are they?" she asked Lang.

"They'll heal."

More good news. The day was full of such. "How long?"

Lang shrugged. "You know burns, but I wouldn't think more than three weeks. But you ask Dr. Phelps what he thinks."

She certainly would.

Lang left Emma sitting up in bed waiting for the breakfast she couldn't eat. How could she not work for three weeks or more? How would she manage looking after herself?

Boothe stepped into the room carrying the breakfast tray and set it on the table. He removed the lids. "Porridge and bread. Coffee." He breathed in the smell. "Mmm, good."

It took all her self-control to keep from kicking him.

"I expect you want coffee first." He poured in a little milk just the way she liked it and held it to her mouth.

She glared at him and clamped her lips together. She hated being dependent on him. Hated the way it made her feel vulnerable and cherished. Hated it enough to refuse to eat.

He waved the cup back and forth in front of her nose. "Coffee. Smell it?"

The aroma filled her nostrils, sent her taste buds into a frenzy.

"I know how much you like your morning coffee." He held the cup to her mouth.

Her brain demanded satisfaction. Her eyes informed him how much she hated this even as she slurped a long, delicious, satisfying mouthful. She closed her eyes and let that first taste slide down her tender throat. Without letting Boothe see how good it tasted, she took three more swallows.

He put down the cup. "Bread or porridge?"

She was starved. She wanted it all. Every mouthful. Every crumb. "Porridge," she said grudgingly.

He fed her a spoonful. Every time she swallowed, he had another ready. His timing was infallible. His smile never faltered despite her nastiest looks. It irked her he was so nice about this.

Couldn't she get a rise out of him at all?

He slathered strawberry jam on the bread.

She took a huge bite not wanting this to take any longer than necessary.

She regretted it almost immediately as the bread scratched her throat.

"No more," she said when she finally choked down the wretched stuff. "How's Jessie?"

"Cranky."

She read his unspoken message in the quick quirk of his brows that he almost managed to hide. *Like you.* She studied the unfinished bread. She was being unreasonable but seemed powerless to stop herself.

"I want to see him."

"He wants to see you, too. I'll go find a nurse and ask if it's possible."

"It's my hands that are useless. Not my feet."

The annoying man chuckled as he left the room.

Emma still scowled when Lang came back pushing a wheelchair. "Climb aboard."

"There's no reason I can't walk."

Lang laughed. What was the matter with everyone that they kept laughing for no reason whatsoever? "Not until the doctor gives his okay." She parked the chair beside the bed and planted her hands on her hips. "Do you want to see Jessie or not?"

Emma resisted a childish urge to say if

she couldn't have her way and walk she wasn't going, but she had to see Jessie and she choked back her pugnacious spirit. She plopped herself in the chair. "Wheel me away."

They crossed the hall to the children's ward. Jessie lay on his back, his leg suspended over the bed. When he saw Emma, he started to cry.

Ignoring Nurse Lang's order to stay in the chair, Emma rose and leaned over the bed. She couldn't smooth his hair. She couldn't adjust his leg. She couldn't wash his face or help care for him. Her eyes flooded and she wanted to wail. But he was okay. His leg would heal. Ignoring the pain in her hands, keeping them from touching anything, she hugged him with her arms and pressed her face to his cheek. "Jessie." Her throat clogged with tears. "I'm so relieved to see you're okay." All the reassuring words from the nurse, the doctor, even Boothe meant nothing until she'd seen Jessie herself.

"Daddy brought me to the doctor." His voice rang with awe.

"He saved your life." And maybe hers, too.

"You burnt your hands." He rolled his head to look from one side to the other, staring at her bandages.

Emma lifted them like a trophy. "I don't remember doing it."

"You did it saving my son." Boothe's voice grated with emotion.

Emma didn't turn. She didn't want to see gratitude on his face. She'd acted out of love for this child. Her heart swelled with gratefulness that Boothe had taken the necessary steps to get medical help.

At Nurse Lang's urging, she sat down. Parked in a wheelchair with her hands two big useless mitts. As useless as a short bit of thread. She didn't like the feeling one bit.

"Do they hurt?" Jessie asked.

"Not much."

"My leg doesn't, either."

Emma guessed he would put on a brave face to convince them all.

She turned to Boothe. "He'll be okay."

"Thanks to you."

"And you." In that silent acknowledgment between them, something strong and solid forged.

She jerked her gaze away. Strong, solid? Hardly. Temporary and pretend.

"Will you stay with me?" Jessie asked.

"As long as I can." She'd stay forever if she could, but forever was not hers to give.

"I'll leave you fifteen minutes," Nurse Lang said. "Then I think both patients should rest."

Emma wanted so much to hold Jessie's hand, smooth his hair. She couldn't so she impotently listened to Jessie recite the horrors of the accident while Boothe leaned over his son and did the things Emma ached to do.

As if reading her frustration, he squeezed her shoulder, rubbing his thumb along her collarbone in a rhythm matching the way he stroked Jessie's head. Comforted, connected to the pair, she rested an arm along Jessie's side.

Nurse Lang returned, took her back to her room and settled her in bed. Emma fought the massive weariness that left her teary, but she lost the battle and fell into a deep sleep.

When she woke, she saw Boothe at her bedside, his head bowed. Sighed deeply and fell asleep again.

For three days she could do nothing but sleep and make quick visits to Jessie courtesy of one of the nurses or Boothe.

She endured having everything done for her. Ada and Sarah helped the nurses but more often than not, Boothe appeared at mealtime.

She tried being rude. Not that she had to try very hard. She was petty and cranky without trying. But nothing deterred his good humor. She wanted only to escape somewhere and be alone. Because, heaven help her, she counted the minutes to mealtime. Listened for his footsteps down the hall. She'd even sunk so low as to resent the time he spent with Jessie.

He never mentioned her confession about Sid, so maybe he thought it was only senseless ramblings. All the more reason for the growing resentment burning inside her chest.

How would she cope when this was over?

He would stop pretending he cared about her. She would have to go on with her life, pretending she didn't care about him. She couldn't imagine how she'd do it. Her impatience mounted until it ruled her world. Four days later, she spoke to the doctor on his morning visit.

"Dr. Phelps, I want to go home. I can manage with help from Ada and Loretta." She'd seen her hands. Knew it would take time for them to heal. She knew, too, that Jessie would be confined to bed for several weeks. Boothe would no doubt spend his time at the hospital with Jessie. At home, she could get peace.

Dr. Phelps considered her request for a long time. Finally he nodded. "Your restlessness isn't doing you any good. Perhaps you would do better at home. I'll speak to the ladies and make sure they're prepared for your care."

"Today?"

"The end of the week at the earliest."

Charlotte came to visit that afternoon. Emma lifted her hands out of the way as her friend hugged her. "I came as soon as I heard."

Emma held her close. "It's so good to see you."

Charlotte wiped tears from her eyes as she edged back. "What can I do to help?"

"Put my hair up."

Charlotte laughed. "You're asking the wrong person. I've always preferred it down. It's beautiful. Like woven gold." Her eyes sparkled. "I'll bet Boothe likes it this way."

Exactly why Emma wanted it up. Several times she'd caught Boothe staring at her hair, knew he stroked it on her pillow when he thought she was sleeping. And her fickle heart loved it.

She did not need anything more she'd have to forget when this was over.

Charlotte pulled a brush from the bedside table. "I'll brush it." Her touch soothed away tension that had crept up Emma's skin making her scalp taut.

"You're a real hero. Everyone is singing your praises. They say you wouldn't let Boothe take Jessie until he promised to take him to the doctor. You really are a spunky gal."

"I just did what had to be done."

"You risked your life." Charlotte's voice caught. She put away the brush and came around the bed to face Emma. "I am so grateful to our good Lord that you're going to be all right."

Emma's heart smote her. "I've forgotten to be grateful," she whispered. She'd been far too consumed with anger at her helpless state, fighting too hard to resist Boothe's help, disgusted with her weakness in telling him about Sid's accident. *Lord, forgive me.* "I've been grumpy and unbearable."

"It's understandable. You've been through a lot and you're in pain."

The pain in her hands was nothing compared to the pain in her heart. Which, without a doubt, would get worse when the pretense was over.

"I've allowed myself to dream of impossible things."

Charlotte looked amused. "I suppose Boothe is somewhat distracted by Jessie's needs right now, but it doesn't mean he cares any less for you."

266

If only it were so, but she couldn't stand to deceive her friend any longer. "Charlotte, there is something I must tell you." *Our love is only a pretense.* But it was real on Emma's behalf. What was the truth? That Emma had bought herself a world full of sorrow in the days to come.

"Here he is now," Charlotte whispered.

Emma, her back to the door, stiffened as she heard his footsteps.

He strode around the bed to face her. He was furious. She couldn't imagine why.

"Is what I hear true?"

"Depends on what you heard."

Charlotte shifted back from the towering man.

"You're pressuring the doctor to let you leave?"

"Aren't you the one who thinks hospitals are unnecessary?"

He dismissed her question with a short grunt. "Who is going to care for you at home?"

Charlotte touched Emma's shoulder. "You can come home with me. I'd love to take care of you. It's what I do best — look after people."

Emma considered the offer. It was tempting. She could escape the necessity of seeing Boothe every day.

"You can't go way out there. I forbid it."

"You *forbid* it? What gives you the right to order me about?"

"We are to be married, in case you've forgotten."

She narrowed her eyes. Who was he trying to convince? They both knew their engagement wasn't real. And she didn't care to deceive Charlotte anymore. "I have forgotten nothing. Have you?"

He managed to look slightly uncomfortable.

"And if you think marriage would give you the right to order me about —"

Charlotte sighed. "If you'll excuse me. I have no desire to see you two fight." She paused at the door. "Remember, after the fighting comes the kissing."

Emma waited until Charlotte left. The two other women who shared the ward were gone, one for a bath and the other for an X ray so she didn't hesitate to turn the full blast of her fury on Boothe. "How dare you come in here and order me about acting like you have some right. Our pretend engagement gives you no such right or obligation."

She wished she could cross her arms to emphasize her point, but her bandages made it impossible.

He glowered at her. "This has nothing to do with our so-called engagement."

"Really. What does it have to do with, if I might be so bold as to ask?"

Boothe's expression faltered.

Emma's lungs felt as if she lay under the weight of another wall. Would he say it mattered? That it was more than pretend? But what difference would it make? She would never be free to marry and have a family. Truth was, she already had a family and would be caring for them the rest of her life.

Pain attacked her heart, raced through her body and settled in her hands. She groaned and lowered her gaze to her swaddled hands.

"Lie down," Boothe ordered, holding back the covers. She did so without hesitation. He grabbed two pillows and put them at her sides. "Now put your hands on these. Keep them elevated."

"When did you become a nurse?" She meant to sound annoyed but her voice came out weak and needy.

"I'm no nurse but I can manage to offer comfort. Between you and Jessie, I'm getting quite good at it in fact."

"How is Jessie?" The pain eased and she managed to fill her lungs.

"He's got some pain. They gave him

something for that." Boothe sucked in air. "I can't imagine him lying in that bed for weeks."

She looked at him closely, trying to see him without the filter of her own needs and desires. He looked weary and yet peaceful. He met her gaze steady and calm.

"You aren't really going out to Charlotte's, are you?"

Did he want her to stay? Did he need her? If only —

There was no room for such thoughts.

She shook her head. "I can't. The doctor wants to keep an eye on my hands."

"Good. I'll feel much better with you here. I'm counting on your help amusing Jessie."

For a whisper of time she'd imagined he would say something else. Something —

He only cared because of Jessie.

She turned away to stare at the door, wishing Charlotte to return and save her from useless, impossible, wonderful dreams.

"Tell Jessie I'll be over to visit him soon."

Boothe rose. "Thank you. For everything."

She closed her eyes as he left. She didn't want thanks. She wanted what she couldn't have.

Lord, God, You have assigned me my path. Only in obeying You and following Your direction can I find true happiness. She knew it, believed it with her whole heart, but never before had it felt so difficult. *I can't do this without Your help. My heart is being rebellious even though I want nothing more than to be cheerfully obedient.*

CHAPTER FOURTEEN

Boothe fled Emma's room. The hospital walls closed in. He grabbed his coat and hat and headed outside.

Why did life have to be so complicated? He wanted to quickly and quietly end this farce with Emma. Spare himself the agony of seeing her every day, wanting to hold her and comfort her, knowing their pretend engagement didn't give him the right.

Boothe's stride lengthened. He turned down Main Street and headed for the lawyer's office.

Ashby glanced up as Boothe barged through the door. He rose and held out his hand. "Sorry to hear about your problems. How are the invalids?"

"Mending." Boothe yanked his hat off and scrubbed a hand over his head. The lawyer didn't know the half of it. "Is everything ready for the judge?"

"I sent him the statements, and he's

requested depositions from your employer, the pastor and several close friends to substantiate your claim that you are gainfully employed and planning marriage."

Boothe nodded. Good thing he and Emma had kept their pretense to themselves. Several times she'd begged to be honest with Aunt Ada and Charlotte.

"Can you give me some names of people to contact?"

Boothe named Charlotte, Aunt Ada, Pastor Douglas and the residents of the boardinghouse.

"I'll take care of things. We should know in a couple weeks how the judge will rule."

Cold sweat trickled down Boothe's spine. He'd done everything he could. Yet he still felt like his hands were tied with cords of steel. "Is there a chance he'll rule in their favor?"

Ashby sighed. "I wish I could say no but I can't with certainty. If your brother-in-law hears of the accident and your son's injuries, he might use it against you."

Boothe jolted to his feet. "How could I be blamed for that?"

Ashby pulled on the cuffs of his suit coat. "I hope you won't be. Not even by insinuation. Now leave this to me, and I'll get the papers prepared and off. That's about all we can do."

Boothe strode from the office, his insides on fire. He couldn't lose Jessie. Yet what more could he do? He needed a miracle.

He slowed. Pastor Douglas said no one deserved a miracle yet God still sent them. Boothe turned in the direction of the church and slipped into the icy interior. He perched on a pew near the front ignoring how the cold wood bit into the back of his legs. For the first time in over two years, he poured out his needs to God.

A few minutes later, he left the building resolved to do his part and trust God to do His. Boothe's number one concern was Jessie. He would do whatever it took to keep his son and see him well and strong and happy.

Emma was necessary both for Jessie remaining with Boothe and for his healing and happiness.

Which meant he had to keep Emma in his life for however long it took. He would hide his love. He would not let her guess how he felt. After her confession about Sid's accident and how she blamed herself, he understood she would never abandon her family. He knew only a breath of regret before he acknowledged his admiration of her dedication. If things were different, he might have been the recipient of that same dedication.

For now he had to get her to promise not to tell anyone their engagement wasn't real.

He returned to the hospital and went directly to her room. Her face bore the ravages of pain. He guessed she'd had her bandages changed. He hurried over and cradled her in his arms.

Emma closed her eyes but not before he saw the way she searched his gaze for something. Whatever it was she wanted — strength, comfort, company — he vowed he would be there to provide it.

He made shushing noises. The same sound he used to comfort Jessie. A tear formed a perfect bead at the edge of her lashes. He stifled a moan and kissed away each drop.

She sniffed. "You don't have to pretend. There's no one here."

"I'm not pretending —" He stopped himself before he uttered forbidden words of love. "To care."

Her eyelids fluttered but she refused to look at him.

He should be grateful because he feared he would not have been successful in hiding his true feelings. He touched her forehead. "You look flushed. I hope you aren't getting a fever."

"I'm fine."

"I've spoken to Ashby. He has to get statements from our friends and Pastor Douglas, affirming we are really and truly engaged. You didn't tell Charlotte the truth, did you?"

He waited. If she had, it would all be for nothing.

She gave a crooked little smile. "I thought of it but no, I didn't say anything." She met his gaze openly. "I have not told anyone the truth."

He didn't want her to go home. It suited him to have her at the hospital so he could pop over from her bedside to Jessie's and back. So he and Emma could sit at Jessie's bedside together.

But she insisted. Dr. Phelps allowed her to return to the boardinghouse after eight days in the hospital. Eight days in which Boothe's opinion of medical personnel was totally and completely revised. He'd seen nothing but genuine care and concern.

Having Emma at home was not as bad as Boothe expected. She had to go to the hospital for daily dressing changes. He went every day and took her in the car Mr. White lent him. Mr. White had been glad to accommodate Boothe's need to spend part of the day with Jessie and let him put in six hours before lunch. Boothe would never have guessed how precious those few minutes together in the car were. Something about the small space created a feeling of intimacy. Emma must have experienced the same thing because she shared flashes of personal information.

"Did I really tell you about Sid?" she asked one day, her voice low, her gaze riveted to her hands.

"You told me about him falling and being hurt."

"He was buried alive."

At the tightness in her voice, he squeezed her shoulder. "No need to blame yourself." He couldn't understand her continuing guilt.

She shrugged away from his touch. "I could have stopped him. He always listened to me. But I didn't want to ruin his fun." She sucked in a whistle of air. "I don't know why I'm even talking about this. I've never told anyone. Not even my parents. I feel bound by my promise to Sid to not tell Mother and Father."

"He was old enough to know how foolish it was."

"I was older."

"Neither of you could have guessed what

would happen."

"We'd been warned. I ignored the warnings."

Boothe rubbed the back of his neck. It did nothing to ease the frustration giving him a headache. "Emma, I understand your feeling of responsibility toward your family, but I simply don't buy this burden of guilt."

She gave him a squinty-eyed look. "How would you feel if Jessie had been buried under that building? And you had to stand by helpless to do anything. Stopped by hands stronger than yours?" She didn't give him a chance to answer. Not that he could speak past the pain of imagining such a terrible event. "Exactly. Would you ever be able to forgive yourself for not fighting harder? Not knowing what to do when they pulled him out?" She shuddered. "I will never forget that feeling of helplessness. I will spend the rest of my life making up for it."

He sighed, reached out to touch her but pulled back when she shied away. "I wish you could find healing."

Purposely misunderstanding him, she glanced at her hands. "They're doing well."

"I will pray for you." He laughed at the way she gaped at him. "I discovered how important and alive my faith was when you and Jessie were unconscious. When only

God could help, I had no trouble turning to Him." He chuckled again, just because he felt so good and right inside. "I know I don't deserve all His blessings, but you do. I'll pray you'll find exactly what you need."

She harrumphed.

But something developed between them at that moment. A connection as strong as steel, as fragile as spiderwebs.

And after that it became easier to talk of their childhoods. She told hair-raising stories about life in the nurses' residence. They shared bits of their dreams and their frustrations. Yet always, there was a constraint between them. He couldn't be totally honest because he couldn't share the emotion overshadowing all others — his love for her. Several times he came close, but it would be unfair to mention it when she'd made it clear from the beginning there could never be anything between them but pretense.

He could only trust God to bear him through the pain when it came time to end this.

Three weeks after the accident Emma's bandages had come off except for a spot on her right hand. She could finally feed herself. But Dr. Phelps warned she wouldn't be able to go back to work for a few weeks yet. She hated being idle as much as she hated being dependent on others, but her biggest concern was her family. She would have no wages to send them this month.

She'd had Charlotte write them a letter explaining her accident.

Boothe brought the mail home and handed her a letter.

She opened it and read Mother's usual weather report. "Wind. More wind. Some snow." Then, "The government wants to buy our land and the surrounding farms to create a wildlife preserve. Father is anxious to sign the deal. We will get enough money to buy a house in town. Father thinks he will be able to find work once the Depression ends. We'll be able to manage without your wages. Now you can begin your own life with Boothe and Jessie. What a sweet boy.

"We have a little house picked out. The one behind the general store. It's much like our home. We figure if we move all our stuff, and arranged it the same way it will seem like home to Sid." Emma knew the house, tucked away behind businesses and between two bigger houses. It did have a familiar design to it. *Lord, help Sid adjust to this move.*

She folded the pages of the letter and

returned it to the envelope. She was free. She could dream of a future. Her engagement didn't have to be pretend.

Boothe sat across from her reading a letter. Suddenly he whooped.

Emma jumped.

"The judge ruled in my favor. Vera and Luke cannot have Jessie. Yahoo!"

Emma was glad for Jessie and Boothe but didn't feel up to cheering. This meant the pretending was over.

He dropped the letter and pulled his chair to her side. He took her wrist and turned her hands over to examine them carefully. They were reddened and scarred, and she wanted to hide them. But she let them remain in his palms wondering what he saw, what he wanted.

Still clasping her hands gently, he looked into her eyes. "Emma, I know this is as far as our agreement goes. You've played along very well and I thank you. That's twice I owe my son to you."

She watched him without speaking. In his mind it was always about Jessie.

"I have one more request. It's a lot to ask but . . ." He paused then rushed on. "Can we still be engaged?"

Her breath stuck somewhere behind her heart as she waited, trying to think what he meant. Did he intend to tell her he wanted more real and less pretend?

"Jessie will be in the hospital a few more weeks. He looks forward to your visits so much. I fear how it would set him back if we told him the truth now. So can we continue as we are a while longer?"

She wanted so much more than pretense. From the first time she saw him across the street, she'd had this impossible dream. Impossible because of her family. Now perhaps — just perhaps — it was possible. Or maybe she was jumping to conclusions. She didn't know if the sale of the farm would net her parents enough to live on. And Sid was still Sid. He'd need care the rest of his life.

Yes, there were still a lot of uncertainties, but there was no reason she couldn't pretend a bit longer.

He mistook her hesitation for not wanting to continue their relationship. "Has it been so hard to be engaged to me?"

No. And that was the problem. It grew increasingly harder to remind herself it wasn't real. Since the accident, Boothe had changed. It was easy for her to think his care was sincere. But it was only about Jessie. "You'll have to tell him the truth at some point."

"I will. When he's stronger."

"All right. We can pretend a bit longer."

He rose slowly. "Good."

Well, she must say he didn't sound happy even though it was his idea.

But over the next days she didn't mind the pretense. They continued to visit Jessie at the hospital. Together they helped him with his lessons and did their best to amuse him. He chafed at being stuck in bed, but on the whole, he did well. She reminded herself over and over that the continued engagement was for Jessie's sake. But she didn't deceive herself. She wanted a few more days of this relationship, too. Even pretend was better than nothing.

Another letter came from home.

"Sid is very happy living in our new house. He's started to go out. I think the closeness of the other buildings makes him feel safe. Last week, he got a job working at the store. He stocks shelves and sweeps and cleans. He seems to be improving right before our eyes."

Emma folded away the letter. Thankfully Boothe was not home and could not see her happy smile and perhaps ask its cause. She hurried upstairs to her room and fell on her knees. *Lord, God, this is such wonderful news.*

More than I could ever think to ask or dream. Sid working and improving. Thank You a hundred times over. She rested her forehead on her hands and sorted through the thoughts tickling at the edges of her mind.

For the first time in eight years, she had no one who needed her, no one who depended on her. Sid was growing up, becoming independent. She should be happier.

She loved Jessie. Wanted to be part of his life for a long time, not just until his leg healed.

She loved Boothe. But he would no longer need her.

Boothe and Jessie belonged here. Perhaps Boothe would take over the boardinghouse. Pain shafted through her. It would have driven her to her knees if she wasn't already there. She couldn't imagine seeing him day after day, continually hiding her love. She had to move on. Somehow. Somewhere. She'd stopped looking for another job since her accident, but now it was time to proceed with that plan. Yes, that's what she'd do.

She buried her face in her hands. She didn't cry. Her sorrow went too deep for tears. It scalded a place all it's own deep in her heart. The wound would never heal. The pain would never die.

"Lord, only with Your help can I move on.

Send Your strength and healing into my heart. And if it is Your will . . ." She could hardly bring herself to pray the words. "Let Boothe see me as more than someone to help Jessie. Help him see me as someone to love."

She remained on her knees for a long time, pouring out her heart to God, encouraged by Scripture verses that came to mind. Peace filled her heart. God was faithful even when His people did foolish things.

She rose, tidied her hair and went downstairs to help Ada finish supper.

A smile curved her lips as Betty and Sarah came in. It remained firmly in place when Ed and Don returned from work. It faltered only slightly when Boothe hurried in from his stay at the hospital. Emma had been there earlier and left him helping Jessie with homework.

"Jessie hoped you'd come back," Boothe said, his voice more curious than scolding.

"I needed to take care of a few things."

He nodded, waiting, his gaze inquiring.

She didn't provide any more details. Soon he would know nothing of what she did while she would wonder every minute what he and Jessie were doing; how they were feeling.

"I'll go in and read to him at bedtime."

She hoped to go by herself. She wanted to walk. She needed to start pulling back from this relationship, but when she went for her coat, Boothe hurried to join her. She could hardly tell him not to come, but he did agree to walk rather than drive.

The night was so still that she could hear the crack of cold. Acrid coal smoke drifted to her from the house they passed. Gold light poured out of the windows and patched the ground before them.

"You're different," Boothe said.

"Oh? Different than what?" Was it possible he sensed her withdrawal from him?

He paused in a spot of light and studied her. "Has something happened?"

Her heart gave a mighty kick. *Tell him. Tell him about the sale of the farm. About Sid getting a job. Tell him how you really and truly feel about him.*

But her pride forbade it. He'd been clear about what this engagement was. Never had he uttered so much as one word to indicate he'd changed his mind. She'd spare them both the embarrassment of pouring out her feelings.

"I suppose I'm anxious to get back to work." That part was completely true.

He didn't pressure her for more details. In fact, he seemed unusually quiet as they went up the steps into the hospital. Perhaps he wondered how he would tell Jessie the truth when this was over.

She stumbled.

Boothe grabbed her, steadied her. "You all right?"

"Just slipped." Her whole world tilted. How would she say goodbye to Jessie? How did you forget a child you'd grown to love?

Two bittersweet days later, Emma struggled to capture her emotions and lock them into carefully guarded drawers. It was proving a difficult task. She ached every minute she couldn't be with Boothe and Jessie and began to look forward to the end so she could move on. Surely it would be easier to deal with her feelings if she didn't have to face them every day.

Today she purposely arrived at the hospital while Boothe was still at work. She checked Jessie's arithmetic questions and tried to get him to concentrate on his reading.

"My leg is almost better."

"I know. You've done so well. Can you read this page to me?"

He glanced at the reader and as quickly looked back at her. "Miss Emma, when are we going to be a real family?"

Emma tapped the reader. "Schoolwork,

young man." No way was she going to lie to this child, promise him things she couldn't deliver. But neither did she plan to be the one to tell him the truth. That would fall on Boothe's shoulders.

Jessie's glance darted past Emma. "Daddy."

Good. Let Boothe deal with these questions.

Boothe squeezed Emma's shoulder and smiled at her. She took that touch and that glance, unlocked the secret drawer and slid them inside. She would not throw away the key yet. She'd allow herself the pleasure of examining a few memories when things got too hard to bear.

Boothe held out a parcel. "For Mr. Jessie Wallace. Someone has sent you a present."

"First time I got real mail."

Emma recognized Mother's handwriting then Jessie tore open the package.

"A coloring book." He flipped through the pages. "Just what I always wanted."

"There's a letter, too." Boothe handed him the page that fell from the wrappings.

"It's from Sid." He showed the letter to them.

Emma's eyes stung. To her knowledge, Sid had never written a thing since his accident.

"Help me read it," Jessie said.

Emma waited for Boothe to do so but he nodded at her. Through the sheen of tears she read:

dr jse
I sen yu this bok. Hop yu lik it. I hav job at stor. I ern mony. I lik it. we sel frm and liv in nu hus in toun. I lik it vry muc. Whn I see yu gain?

Luv Sid

Emma faltered and swallowed hard.

Jessie took the letter. "I like Sid. When can we see him again?"

"They've moved?" Boothe sounded angry. "Sid is working?" His voice deepened.

He moved away, went to the other side of the bed. His gaze seared her skin. She couldn't, wouldn't look at him. He had no reason to be angry. Their agreement did not include promising to share every detail of their lives. Even as she thought it, her heart denied it. Not because of any promise but because every corner of her wayward heart wanted to belong to Boothe — her secrets, her fears, her dreams and most of all, each and every beat for the rest of her life.

CHAPTER FIFTEEN

Boothe's stomach boiled with acid. The one thing he'd admired in Emma, counted on, was she could be trusted. How wrong could he be? Her parents had sold the farm and moved to town and she didn't think it bore mentioning? And now Sid had a job? Why hadn't she told him?

Because hiding behind her parents' and Sid's needs had become her protection against feeling anything real.

She couldn't have made it any plainer that she didn't want anything but pretense between them. Well, no more of it. From here on out it was honesty.

Jessie was strong enough to deal with the truth.

His anger abated. Jessie would be hurt.

Boothe stiffened his spine. He had no one but himself to blame, but he'd do it all over again if that's what it took to keep his son.

He admired Jessie's coloring book. He

hoped he responded correctly to questions and comments. Emma, gratefully, had sense enough to be quiet.

He could hardly wait to get her alone and confront her.

"I'll give you a ride," he said, when it came time to leave.

"I don't mind walking."

"The car is here." His tone must have conveyed he would stand no argument. She meekly put on her coat and accompanied him to the automobile.

He waited until she settled in the seat beside him then faced her. "When did you plan to tell me your news?"

"Exactly what news do you mean?" Her eyes warned him she wouldn't be bullied.

"Did your folks sell the farm?"

She nodded.

"And Sid has a job?"

Another nod but not a hint of regret for not relaying this news.

He softened his voice, hoping it would have more effect. "Why didn't you tell me?"

"What difference does it make? Jessie is about to be discharged. Our pretense is about to end. I am applying for a job in North Dakota. I doubt we'll see each other again."

She said it with such hard certainty that it

made him want to grind his teeth and spit out fragments.

"You didn't say anything because you no longer have anything to hide behind."

She quirked an eyebrow.

"Sid has always been your protection against letting yourself care about anyone. Now what excuse will you use? To think I felt sympathy for your plight. I prayed God would provide a way out for you." His snort of laughter was self-mocking. "Don't look so surprised. Yes, I prayed."

"Then it seems God has answered your prayers."

The fury left him. He leaned over the steering wheel. "Somehow I thought it would feel better."

"Really. What did you expect would happen? Why did you pray?"

He'd prayed so he would be free to love Emma. She obviously didn't feel the same way or she wouldn't have hidden this news. The acid returned to his stomach and burned like wildfire. "I wanted you to be free of your guilt and responsibility. But I see you never will be. You'll just find something else to become your shining badge of 'ought.' "

She opened the door. "I think I prefer to walk home in the fresh air." She stepped out and shut the door quietly but firmly.

He let her go. He couldn't deal with his raging emotions. He drove away, heading the opposite direction of the boardinghouse. He needed time to think.

He'd been so noble. Honored her commitment to her family. Poured out his affection without once admitting his love. Surely she had seen how hard it was to keep back the words.

Cold seeped through his bones, cooled his marrow. His anger died. He turned the car around and headed back. As he passed the church, he pulled over and stopped.

When all else fails, turn to God.

Jesus never fails.

God, You answered my prayer to relieve Emma of her responsibilities. And here I am angry about it. You know that isn't the reason I'm so upset, though.

Why was he so angry?

Because his trust had been shattered.

But had it?

What reason did Emma have to share her news with him? They'd both agreed this engagement was only until Jessie was better.

God, I'm in a pickle here. I don't want to lose her. How do I show her I want to make this real?

He had to start over. They'd break off this

farce, and then he would court her for real. He'd show her how much he cared.

Back at the boardinghouse, he took a deep breath and held it until he felt in control. For a few more days he had to keep his love hidden. Just until Jessie got home. There'd be no more need for pretending. Then he'd show Emma how much he loved her.

He went inside. Emma stood in front of the stove, helping Aunt Ada with supper. Aunt Ada looked tired. Boothe tried to do as much as he could to help, but with Jessie in the hospital . . .

He would start over on a number of levels as soon as Jessie was discharged. It would take all his self-control to keep his feelings hidden until then, but he was determined to do this right.

Today was the day. Jessie was getting out of traction. Boothe wanted to be present for it, but Dr. Phelps said he didn't want a parent hanging about. So he put in his short day at work, forcing himself to do each chore carefully while his insides curled and knotted and twisted. Today he would take Jessie home. Today he would tell the truth about his engagement to Emma — that he didn't want it to end. And then he could begin his honest, heartfelt courtship of Emma. He closed his eyes and allowed himself to think of the pleasure of taking her for long walks, telling her all the things he had stored in his heart.

He yanked on his coat and hat and hurried to the hospital. He rushed into the children's ward and jerked to a stop. Jessie seemed so small without his leg suspended, without pulleys. He barely made a bump under the covers.

Boothe wanted to scoop his son into his arms and hold him like he hadn't been able to since the accident. He moved closer, saw Jessie's face wet with tears and was at his side in three strides. "What's wrong? Did it hurt? What can I do?"

"Not my leg," Jessie choked out.

"Then what? Tell me and I'll fix it."

"You can't."

"I'll try."

Jessie rolled his head back and forth.

Boothe wondered what had upset him. Was it just a reaction to knowing he could go home? "I thought Emma would be here." Dr. Phelps had said she could come in as soon as the traction was removed.

"She was." Jessie's voice wobbled, and a fresh flood of tears slid down his cheeks.

Boothe grabbed a hankie and wiped away the moisture. "Did she have to go somewhere?"

Jessie nodded and sucked in a noisy gulp of air. "She's gone."

"She'll be back."

"No. She said she wouldn't."

Bony fingers clawed up Boothe's spine. "What do you mean? Where's she gone?"

"She went home. She said you would explain."

Home? She'd left? Without a word? How could he tell her how he felt now?

Jessie gave Boothe a look rife with accusation then let out a gusty wail. He choked out a hiccuped sentence. "I want Emma back."

So do I, son. So do I. Boothe glanced at the clock on the end wall. "She's going on the afternoon train?"

"Ye-es."

"I'll persuade her to stay. I'll have to leave you here while I go get her. Are you okay?"

Jessie's expression brightened. "You'll get her?"

"If I hurry."

"You tell her to come back. You tell her I want her to be my mommy." Suddenly he narrowed his eyes. "You tell her I love her."

Boothe chuckled. "I'll be sure to tell her." And he'd tell her for himself, too.

He hurried from the room. He had just

enough time to catch the train before it left.

Dr. Phelps stopped him in the hall. "Jessie did very well. Like I said, he'll have to work up to full activity gradually. But as long as he's careful —"

"Doc, I gotta go. I'll talk to you when I get back."

Dr. Phelps's mouth dropped open as Boothe rushed out the door.

Boothe headed for the train station, his heart ticking away each departing second. He had to make it —

"No." He braked. A wagon had tipped over on the ice, blocking the road. Half a dozen men struggled to untangle the horse. Several more worked to right the wagon and reload the goods.

He couldn't wait. Even as he turned the automobile around, he heard the train whistle. Ignoring the surprised glances of people he almost ran down, he drove as fast as he could for the railway.

He rounded the corner. The caboose was several hundred yards down the tracks. He dismissed the need to go to the station, turned a sharp left and raced after the train. It pulled farther away with every puff of smoke. Boothe slowed for a man crossing the street with a loaded wheelbarrow. Then a woman waddled across, her arms overflowing with parcels. The train pulled farther and farther away. He would never catch it. Why had he not told Emma how he felt? Why had he thought it made sense to wait?

Lord, I am so dense sometimes. Please give me another chance with her, and I promise I will be completely honest. I love her. Suddenly, he laughed. God had sent this woman into his life. She was exactly what both Jessie and he needed. God help him, he only hoped he hadn't ruined his chances with her.

He returned to the hospital.

Jessie pushed up on his elbows and looked past Boothe. "Where is she?"

"I missed the train."

Jessie fell back. "You let her go. You're mad at her. That's why she was sad."

"She was?" His heart beat a little more smoothly thinking she might regret her decision to leave.

"She pretended she wasn't but I could tell."

He knew what he had to do. "I'm going to catch the next train. It isn't until morning." The early train he and Jessie had taken to accompany Emma home for Christmas. "It means you'll have to stay here for another day or two while I go to her."

Jessie grinned. "I don't mind so long as

298

you bring her back."

Boothe nodded. He only hoped Emma would give him another chance. Somehow he would convince her how much he loved her. He'd beg on hands and knees if he had to.

It's over. It's over. Every clack of the tracks reverberated with the words.

Emma forced her attention to the passing scenery though she couldn't have reported one detail of what she saw. She'd known from the beginning that this day would come. But she could never have imagined the way her insides writhed with pain, the way her brain felt fragile and brittle, nor the way her limbs turned to wooden foreign objects.

Yet it was time to move on. No matter how difficult.

She'd visit her family. See their new home. Make sure they really and truly were doing well and didn't need her.

Her throat tightened so she couldn't even swallow the tears clogging it. Her family didn't need her. Boothe no longer needed her. Jessie would soon enough forget her. She didn't even have a job. She'd left a letter on her matron's desk informing her of her resignation effective immediately. She hoped an opening in North Dakota would work out. Until then . . .

God, I don't know where I belong. Nor what You want me to do. Show me. Guide me.

She settled her thoughts on God's faithfulness and let peace seep through her body, easing her mind and relaxing her limbs.

I love Boothe. I wish it were mutual.

The train pulled in to the Banner station and she climbed down, her bag in hand. The rest of her things remained back at Ada's boardinghouse. She'd send for them as soon as she had a job.

"Come to see how your folks is doing?" Mr. Boushee called when he saw her. "I was some surprised when they decided to move into town. Heard they got a nice price for that farm. And Sid. Well, who ever expected him to be so useful? Best thing ever happened to him was getting off that farm. You run along now and see for yourself." He waved her toward the street.

Emma hurried away glad the man hadn't asked questions. She had no answers to give anyone. Not even herself.

She crossed the street and went down a block then stopped before the house Dad had purchased. It felt strange to think this was home now.

She took a deep strengthening breath and

headed for the door, eased it open and called, "Mother, Father?"

Mother hurried into the hallway. "Emma. What a surprise."

"You're the ones full of surprises. Not a hint that you might be wanting to sell."

Mother fluttered her hands. "It all happened so suddenly. We didn't have time to tell anyone. It was unexpected though we'd heard rumors about the wildlife preserve." She took Emma's coat and hung it in the closet.

"Show me the house."

It was a house very like the one on the farm — a big comfortable kitchen, a small orderly front room, a small room that served as a sewing room and storage. Upstairs, four bedrooms. One had her familiar things. Yet it didn't feel familiar. She stood in the doorway looking at the quilt that had been on her bed as long as she remembered and let an ache wrap around her heart and flood through her veins. Emma didn't belong here. She didn't know where she belonged.

"Come to the kitchen and I'll make tea," Mother said.

"Where's Dad?" Emma followed her down the stairs and into the kitchen, full of furniture from the farm that she'd known all her life. But it all felt different.

"Well, that's another piece of unexpected good news. You know how he's always been good with numbers?" Mother waited for Emma's nod. "The government agency needed someone to keep track of the transactions on behalf of the preserve. They practically begged your father to do it." Mother shook her head, her face wreathed in disbelief. "We never expected things to turn out this way. We thought we'd have to stay on the farm for Sid's sake. This is so much better." She took a long breath. "God is good."

Emma nodded. "I can't believe Sid has a job. Does he really go on his own? What does he do?"

"He'll be home soon, and he'll tell you all about it. In fact, he'll probably want to take you tomorrow and show you what he does. Mr. MacKenzie says he's a great help and always so pleasant."

Emma couldn't remember the last time she'd seen her mother so animated.

As soon as they'd finished tea, Mother took her to the sewing room. "I'm making a quilt from the old trousers and things I sorted out at the farm."

"Mother, you haven't made a quilt since . . ." Since Sid's accident.

"Seems like we're all finding ways to start over."

"I'm so glad." They looked through the stacks of old clothes, Mother all the time talking about the different quilt tops she could make. Then Emma helped Mother prepare supper.

"Here comes Sid."

Emma hurried to the window. Sid crossed the backyard, swinging his arms. His lips moved. She leaned closer to the pane. "Is he singing?"

Mother laughed softly, pleased. "He sings every day as he walks to and from his job."

"He isn't afraid?" Since his accident, Sid had been afraid of the outdoors.

"He says it's like being inside, the buildings are so close."

"Who'd have thought things would turn out like this?"

"It restores my faith in God."

"Me, too." If God provided for Sid and her parents in ways none of them had ever dreamed of, she could trust Him to do the same for her. *Lord, God, I don't know what You have in mind for me, but I thrust myself into Your care. Guide me into what's next in my life.*

Sid hurried in, still singing, hung his coat and hat. Emma waited and watched from the kitchen door. He saw her and rushed to give her a hug, swinging her off her feet. "Emma, I got a job." He put her down and grinned so wide his ears wiggled.

"I heard. Good for you."

"Yes, good for me. Mr. Mac says I'm his best helper ever."

"I'm sure you are." She blinked back tears at the change in Sid.

Her father returned. He walked more sprightly than he had in years. She could only guess that the farmwork had taken its toll day after day, and now he no longer had that strain, his joints felt better.

Despite her sorrow at having left Boothe and Jessie, Emma rejoiced along with Sid and her parents that evening. "This is how I remember our family," she said later after they'd shared tea and cookies and Dad had read the Bible aloud.

"I remember, too," Sid said. He pushed to his feet. "I'm going to bed. Need my rest to work tomorrow." They heard him singing in his bedroom.

Emma's pleasure at his happiness was marred by the talk she planned to have with her parents.

She waited until Sid called good-night. "Mother, Dad, before you go to bed, there is something I must tell you. It's time I told you the truth." She intended to clear the slate tonight. From this day onward, she would live with no guilty secrets. "I deceived you about Boothe and I being engaged. I did it to make sure Boothe was able to keep Jessie." She explained the situation. "That's over now. The judge ruled in Boothe's favor."

"I'm sorry," Dad said. "He seemed like a good man. I thought he truly cared for you."

Emma nodded, unable to speak for a moment. She sent a prayer for help. "I haven't been honest about something else." She sucked in air that seemed to go no farther than her nose. "Sid's accident."

Mother shook her head. "That's in the past."

"No. I have to tell you the whole story. It's my fault." She told every awful, painful detail. "I'm sorry," she choked out. "I should have stopped him." She hung her head, unable to face the disappointment she knew would be in both her parents' eyes.

"Emma." Father's soft, gentle voice drove her sorrow deeper. They'd endured so many years of hardship because of her neglect. "Emma, we knew what happened."

Her head went up like someone had jerked on a set of reins. Mother nodded. "We've always known Sid disobeyed us."

"I should have stopped him."

Mother gave a short laugh. "Do you really think he would have listened to you? Have you forgotten what a headstrong boy he was?"

"That's why you instructed me to watch out for him." She'd failed miserably.

"No. No." Dad sounded sad. "We didn't expect you to feel responsible for the choices he made. We only meant for you to caution him and try to persuade him to tame that wild spirit of his. Emma, we never once blamed you for Sid's accident. It pains me to think you blamed yourself. You have been the most dutiful daughter one could ask for. We're just so happy that we no longer need your help. You can get on with your own life."

Her parents didn't feel comfortable with expressing their emotions, but tonight she needed healing that could be wrought from their touches and words. She rushed to them, knelt between them and laid her head in Mother's lap. Mother made hushing noises and stroked her hair. Dad patted her back.

"Child, it's time for us all to move on. Thank the good Lord for providing us a way."

A sob rolled up Emma's throat. She

captured it on the back of her tongue and held it there even though it threatened to choke her. She would not cry. She would not take one bit of pleasure from this new beginning for her parents and Sid. If it felt like the end of the world to her, she wouldn't let anyone know. She would trust God.

"It's time to forget the past and look to the future."

Emma let her father's words sift through her thoughts. "Boothe and I had an agreement — our engagement was only pretend until the court date was over." She shuddered. "I guess I forgot to pretend." She sat back on her heels and lifted her twisted face to her parents. "I fell in love with him. Starting over is going to be difficult."

"Emma, I am sorry for your pain." Dad gripped her shoulder. "But even this is not beyond God's help. Perhaps Boothe feels the same way."

Emma shook her head. "He was very honest. This was only about Jessie." She pushed to her feet. "I'm so glad things have turned out well for you and Sid." She wanted to escape to her room. God would help and sustain her. She believed all the right things. If only it would erase the pain. "Good night." She managed to get the words out without any tears escaping.

The sun shone bright, mocking Emma's emotions. She'd spent a restless night struggling to come to grips with her feelings. In the end, she'd fallen asleep exhausted and wakened too weary to think past the next few minutes.

She'd gone with Sid to his job, amazed at his confidence in walking the distance from home to the store. It would seem an insignificant thing to most people but for him to cross the yard and the alley to the back entrance of the store was a major step. When she asked him how he did it, he said Jessie had told him how. "Just don't look." Her throat had clogged at his words.

At the store, he showed her his tasks, amazing her with his confidence and pride. Mr. MacKenzie seemed genuinely pleased with Sid's work. "Once I show him what I want done, he never misses. I like a man I can count on."

Sid stood taller at the praise. "I always do what you say." He grabbed the broom. "I go clean the steps now."

Emma left him to his work. Rather than return home immediately, she decided to wander the main street of Banner hoping the fresh air would clear her thoughts.

Spring was ready to burst forth, but somehow she found no joy in the fact. No anticipation. Nothing but empty dread. She gave herself a mental shake. She needed to get another job. That would give her something to focus on.

She jerked to a stop and stared at the man striding out of the hotel dining room. Boothe? How could that be possible? Had her mind conjured up the very person she'd been thinking about?

She tore her gaze away, let her eyes adjust to the bright sunshine as she stared across the street and focused on the sign above the mercantile store. She slowly allowed her gaze to return to the man adjusting his hat in front of the hotel. "Boothe?"

He turned. His eyes widened. "Emma."

He closed the distance between them in long hurried strides. "I came on the early morning train."

"Why?"

"You didn't say goodbye."

"Was it necessary?" He'd come all this way just to say goodbye?

His eyes grew dark and shadowed as if her words had disappointed him. And then he seemed to find purpose and he smiled so gently, so softly, it brought a sudden glut of tears to the back of her throat.

"It's such a lovely day. Let's walk." He pulled her hand around his arm and pressed her fingers to his forearm. For a moment, his hand lingered on hers.

She allowed herself to enjoy the comfort of his closeness then lifted her chin. She could say goodbye if that's what he wanted. And she could then pick up the pieces of her life and move on — with God's help, His everlasting arms beneath her and the shelter of His wings above.

They walked past stores so familiar to Emma that she didn't need to glance at any sign to know what they sold. The street was short; the selection of businesses were limited, many of them boarded up. Banner was a town struggling for survival. They came to the end of the street and faced the empty prairie.

Emma's heart shriveled inside her chest. She couldn't face the emptiness of the landscape on top of the emptiness of her heart.

Boothe rested gentle hands on her shoulders and turned her to face him.

She couldn't meet his gaze knowing she would be unable to hide her feelings. He'd see. He'd guess.

But he caught her chin with a long, gentle finger and lifted her head.

She closed her eyes, felt moisture clinging to her lashes.

He brushed a fingertip across each closed eye. "You're crying. Why?"

A breath shivered into her lungs. She held it and prayed for strength to endure this final goodbye. "So many things have happened. Sid and Dad both have jobs." Her voice refused to work and she sniffed.

Boothe's finger lingered on her cheek and traveled to her chin. "I'm glad things are working out for them. And you, I suppose." He cleared his throat. "Emma, I think it's time for a little honesty between us."

She jerked open her eyes.

"I mean about our feelings for each other. Or at least my true feelings about you."

Her lungs, her heart, her mind all stopped functioning.

"Emma, I want a chance to start over. To court you like you deserve. To show you I love you."

A distant ticking in her ears warned her she needed to breathe soon or risk fainting. She sucked in air redolent with spring and ringing with the songs of larks and robins.

"Emma, tell me I haven't waited too long." His voice rang with urgency. "Tell me there's a chance you might learn to care for me."

She blinked, tried to find the words to say to express the joy that grew with each beat of her heart. She laughed for the sheer volume of it. "Boothe, if you only knew how hard it's been for me to keep up the pretense of our engagement."

Lines in his face deepened.

She couldn't stand to see him so uncertain, so ready to be hurt. "Boothe, I've loved you since I first saw you."

"I was quite rude. I'm sorry."

"I don't mean when we met in the boardinghouse. I saw you outside. When you bent over and touched Jessie with such tenderness, I knew you were the sort of man I'd dreamed about — tender, able to express your feelings."

He looked so relieved that she wanted to hug him. But as suddenly as his expression had softened, it grew hard again. "I blamed nurses and doctors for Alyse's death. All of them. I was angry and had to blame someone. But after seeing how efficient and caring most of them are, I realized I can't brand them all because of one error. I pray that pair has learned their lesson, but I've forgiven them." He trailed his gaze over her face until she knew she glowed from it. "And one special nurse proved to be so stubborn, so principled, so loving and giving — is it any wonder I asked you to marry me?"

"It was for Jessie."

"It was. But I didn't mind having an excuse."

"And now?"

He chuckled. "I need no excuse. I love you. From your lovely thick hair that you insist on hiding to your giving heart to your practical nature. Say it again."

She knew exactly what he meant. "I love you, Boothe Wallace. For today and all my tomorrows." At the look of sheer wonder on his face, she vowed she would tell him often.

"Emma, I love you so much I can't think there will be enough tomorrows to allow me to show it but I will try."

He lowered his head and kissed her.

She thought it was a good way to start showing his love.

EPILOGUE

Emma raced to pull the burning cookies from the oven. She scooped them off the cookie tray, decided they were too bad to salvage and tossed them in the garbage.

She had to pay closer attention to what she was doing instead of staring out the window watching for Boothe to come home.

She glanced at the clock. Had it stopped? She cocked her head. No. She could hear it ticking. She went into the front room to check the mantel clock. It said the same time.

She returned to the kitchen and dropped cookie dough onto another tray. This time she would stand in front of the oven until they were done.

She forced herself to think about all the good changes she'd been privy to rather than think of the future.

She and Boothe had married a year ago. She loved him more with each day. And he found delightful ways of showing his love for her. He found little gifts for her, brought her bunches of wildflowers, but what she enjoyed most was how he touched her so often. Brushing her hair off her shoulders was the touch she loved the most. She chuckled. She'd finally given in and let her hair hang loose. She'd cut it to mid length so it was more manageable. She loved how Boothe squeezed her shoulder in passing, pressed his hand to the small of her back as they went into a room, how he rested his hand over hers when he read the Bible at supper. She loved those little gestures that said so much more to her than the words.

She checked the cookies again — not quite done — and closed the oven door.

Aunt Ada had insisted Boothe and Emma take over the boardinghouse.

"Loretta and I have had our eyes on that little house next door. Now we can both sit back and enjoy our rocking chairs."

Emma chuckled. Didn't seem to her either of them spent much time in their rocking chairs. They'd made a trip east to visit Aunt Ada's childhood home. They'd spent a few weeks in Victoria, British Columbia, and returned full of praise for the genteel British way of life. And they'd organized a knitting group to make blankets and mittens for the less fortunate.

She pulled the cookies from the oven and filled the kettle with water to make tea. Boothe had promised to be home early today. Mr. White was so good about letting Boothe take time off when he needed to, and today he wanted to be home before Jessie.

She heard his step at the door and hurried to greet him.

He swung her into a long delicious hug then leaned back to look into her eyes. "You're glowing."

"I'm so happy. It's finally happened. We are going to have a baby." It had been the one disappointment to their marriage — her inability to conceive. Until now.

He hugged her again. "I can hardly wait to share a child with you."

She wrinkled her nose. "What do you call Jessie? A pet dog?"

He laughed. "No. He's my pride and joy."

"Mine, too."

"I won't love him any less, but this baby will be the product of our love."

"I could never love Jessie more, but I know what you mean. Do you think he'll be pleased?"

They heard him calling to his friends as he returned from school.

"I think he'll be very happy."

Jessie gave them both a questioning look as he stepped inside. He must have wondered why his father was home and why they grinned like kids on Christmas morning. He'd grown so much. And he seemed content.

"Let's have tea and cookies," Emma said. She served them each a cup, making Jessie's mostly milk.

She sent Boothe a silent message. She couldn't wait.

Boothe held his cup between his hands. "Jessie, we have some news for you."

Jessie stiffened. Emma understood he was still a little fearful that things would change on him.

"We are going to have a baby."

His eyes widened. His mouth rounded. He looked from Boothe to Emma. "A baby?"

"A brother or sister for you," Emma said.

"He'll be your baby, right?"

Emma shook her head. "He'll be *our* baby." She pulled Jessie to her. "Someone for us all to love. Just like we love you and always will."

He nodded. "When is he going to be born?"

"It might be a girl."

317

Jessie waited.

"About Christmastime."

Jessie whooped and laughed. "Just what I wanted."

Boothe and Emma exchanged puzzled looks and then Emma recalled the first Christmas concert when they'd been together, she and Boothe pretending to be engaged, both already in love with the other but afraid to admit it. Thankfully they'd eventually eliminated the pretense. "You asked for a Christmas baby."

Jessie nodded then Boothe wrapped his arms around Emma and Jessie.

"I have been blessed beyond measure," he said. "Thanks be to God."

Emma, her voice muffled by being squished between the other two, managed to say, "His blessings are beyond comprehension."

Dear Reader,

This is a story with many personal elements in it. Both my husband and I have relatives who were born during the Depression and were taken in as children by friends because of economic circumstances, and the parents were powerless to prevent it. We have also personally dealt with an injury and the accompanying guilt, similar to the circumstances of the heroine and her brother. I wrote this story hoping to show how people cope with such challenges. There are no magic answers in my story, just as there are no magic answers in real life. But there is God. He is ever faithful, the great Healer and the righteous Judge. In that I take comfort. In that I find strength and assurance.

My prayer is that you will find the same in the pages of this story and above all that you will be encouraged by the power of love — both human and divine.

I love to hear from readers. If you want to tell me how this story worked for you, send me a message. You can find news about my books and me, plus a contact e-mail address

on my Web site:
www.lindaford.org.

Blessings,
Linda Ford

QUESTIONS FOR DISCUSSION

1. Emma makes her living as a nurse in the local hospital. Was it unusual for a woman in the 1930s to have a profession? Why or why not?

2. Boothe lost his wife because of medical negligence. How does this color his feelings toward doctors and nurses? How does he first react to Emma because she is a nurse?

3. Because of his reduced economic circumstances, Boothe and his son move to South Dakota to help out at his aunt's boardinghouse. How do you think he came to this decision? Do you think it was easy or difficult for him?

4. Emma has a secret she is reluctant to share with anyone. How did that affect her life in general, and particularly her

relationship with Boothe? Do you have secrets that hinder your life and relationships? How do you deal with them?

5. Emma believes she can never marry. Do her reasons make sense? What would you do if you were in her position?

6. In order to make sure the children have Christmas presents, Emma and the boarders work together to create handmade gifts. Have you ever created or donated presents for others? How did it make you feel?

7. Boothe is afraid his son will be taken from him, and believes the only way to prevent it is to marry. Does this seem like a logical solution? Could there be any other way?

8. It takes a serious accident for Boothe and Emma to realize some important truths. What conclusions did they come to? Can you think of a time when it took something serious or scary to make you stop and take stock?

9. Both Boothe and Emma have dealt with harsh realities. Each of them reacts in

unique ways. How do they differ? Are there ways they are similar? How do their disappointments affect their faith?

10. There is a woman in this story who must deal with a profound disappointment — Auntie Vera. How do you feel about what has happened to her? If you could speak to her, what comfort would you offer?

11. Emma's family decides to sell the farm and move to town. Why was this the best thing for everyone, especially her brother, Sid?

12. Above all, this was a love story. How do you feel about Boothe and Emma's romance? Do you think they will live happily ever after? Why or why not?

ABOUT THE AUTHOR

Linda Ford shares her life with her rancher husband, a grown son, a live-in client she provides care for, and a yappy parrot. She and her husband raised a family of fourteen children, ten adopted, providing her with plenty of opportunity to experience God's love and faithfulness. They had their share of adventures as well. Taking twelve kids in a motor home on a three thousand mile road trip would be high on the list. They live in Alberta, Canada, close enough to the Rockies to admire them every day. She enjoys writing stories that reveal God's wondrous love through the lives of her characters.

Linda enjoys hearing from readers. Contact her at linda@lindaford.org or check out her Web site at www.lindaford.org, where you can also catch her blog, which often carries glimpses of both her writing activities and family life.

We hope you have enjoyed this Large Print book. Other Thorndike, Wheeler, Kennebec, and Chivers Press Large Print books are available at your library or directly from the publishers.

For information about current and upcoming titles, please call or write, without obligation, to:

Publisher
Thorndike Press
295 Kennedy Memorial Drive
Waterville, ME 04901
Tel. (800) 223-1244

or visit our Web site at:

http://gale.cengage.com/thorndike

OR

Chivers Large Print
published by BBC Audiobooks Ltd
St James House, The Square
Lower Bristol Road
Bath BA2 3SB
England
Tel. +44(0) 800 136919
email: bbcaudiobooks@bbc.co.uk
www.bbcaudiobooks.co.uk

All our Large Print titles are designed for easy reading, and all our books are made to last.